More comments:

Win/Win Situation
Great warm up
I loved it. I got so wet reading it I had to go get my largest fake cock and sit on it while I diddled my clit. When my husband got home I nearly raped him at the door. After he calmed down he asked what happened and I had saved the story. He read it and took me to bed without supper and we screwed almost all night. And yes I got a sore pussy and sore butt. But I love the story and what it did to us.

  ---A Reader

Holy shit
Un-fucking-believable... I came three times during the story... definitely THE hottest story I have ever read on this site. ---A Reader

Excellent!
What a great fantasy, now I definitely want my husband to act the outlaw in bed!!!!!! ---A Reader

Hotter than Hell
That was fantastic. Really, really hot. By far, I think, the hottest I've read on this site!!! Keep giving it to us!!! ---A Reader

Oh man...
Oh man that was so damn hot... lucky girl, made me wet reading it. Wow! To have a man give it to you and want more after he cums... Wow! ---A Reader

Hot like fire
Oh my God I felt everything she was feeling, then my lover came home and we acted it out. Damn I'm sore but God the sex was good!! Please write more!!!! ---A Reader

I'll Be With You In My Dreams
Sweet dreams!
This was one of the most enjoyable stories that I've read! It truly got my imagination running!   ---A Reader

A Huge One Could Be Yours
Too damn funny...
Absolutely hilarious. :) Great writing.   ---A Reader

Cabin In The Woods
Still throbbing
Just finished reading your story and my pussy is still throbbing! Keep up the good work.   ---A Reader

Royally Fucked
Great story, very real
Seriously, this was fantastic. I loved that there was fucking AND affection. It was hardcore, but very sensual at the same time. Definitely written by a woman. I have one very sexy, amazing black man in my life, but I can't lie that I often dream of two.   -
--A Reader

Every woman's fantasy

I must admit that is my fantasy also. Although I am a black woman, I too am strangely drawn to beautiful black men. The sheer thought of having two big black dicks at once is a wonderful turn on. Keep the great stories coming.   ---A Reader

The Blues Man
A very sweet read
I'm delighted to see such a sweet treatment of both subjects: age and interracial. The care taken to depict the characters as human beings with flaws compliments the quiet sex which eventually happens between the main characters. This was a wonderful read.   -
--A Reader

Balls of Cobalt Blue

And Other Erotica

Short Fiction by Stanfield Major

Acknowledgments

First of all I want to thank all the women who've shared their deepest sexual secrets with me over the years. Otherwise I wouldn't have a clue.

I want to thank Literotica.com. These stories would never have been written without them. Through the forum they provided I found my audience.

My story, I'll Be With You In My Dreams, was published in the online erotic magazine Clean Sheets in 2003.

My story, No, She Said, was included in Erotic Tales, the print anthology published by Justus Roux, in 2003.

I wish to express my gratitude to Jean Marie Stine of Renaissance E Books for her support and encouragement. And for publishing an Ebook edition of this book in 2005.

My story, The Blues Man, was included in The Mammoth Book of Best New Erotica, Volume 6, in 2007. Edited by Maxim Jakubowski.

Contents

I'll Be With You In My Dreams

I've always been a dreamer. More in the sense of having my head so far in the clouds that I couldn't attend to the practical aspects of everyday life than that of having an abundance of the phantasmagoria accompanying sleep. I teach American and English literature so in the former sense of the word my life hasn't been impacted too severely. And, with regard to the latter sense, the truth is that for most of my life I've only remembered bits and pieces of the wondrous flow of images and sensory input that entered my slumbers.

Sometime in the 1970s I read the books of Carlos Castaneda and was attracted to his discussions of dreaming consciously and guiding your dreams. A faint hunger for that kind of experience rumbled below consciousness through the years. Then, almost nine months ago, in a used bookstore, I caught sight of a book by Stephen LaBerge titled Lucid Dreaming and the faint hunger expanded into an aching void. I read the book with care over the period of about a month and then began to practice the techniques.

It was a long tedious haul. There were many times I almost gave up. My forbearing wife, Anita, observed my antics with an amused exasperation. Over the course of our long marriage she's suffered through a multitude of my enthusiasms; some short lived and some extending for years. This one at least, she told me with a short laugh, she could sleep through.

I'd been practicing the techniques described by Dr. LaBerge for a little over four months with minimal success when it happened. At first I thought I was awake. But then, recalling that I'd crossed the room in a fraction of a second, I realized that I'd achieved my goal. I looked at my hands. They glowed in a way I'd never seen before.

I looked toward the window. The late spring sun was peeking over the horizon. In another split second I was outside, floating above the lawn. Now I had the freedom but I didn't know what to do.

I decided to try flying. In an instant I was soaring above the neighborhood. I remembered having these dreams as a kid and how much I'd loved them. I sailed over the house of our neighbors, Hector and Eileen, and I realized I was thinking of Eileen. And there I was in their bedroom. Hector lay sprawled on his back, snoring softly. Eileen was curled in a fetal position, facing away from him. They both were nude.

They'd moved into this house, two doors down from us, almost four years ago. And ever since the day I'd first seen her standing in their driveway wearing a bright yellow dress I'd carried a small torch for her, one with an intense flame. No one knew of this torch. Not Eileen, I was certain. But many times over the years its heat had warmed my heart. Never, until now, had I seen Eileen naked. I liked what I saw. I flitted to her side of the bed and looked down at her sleeping form. I wondered if I was seeing Eileen or was imagining, in my dream state, what she might look like.

Then, with a shock, I realized her eyes were open. They were focused on me. We stared at each other for what seemed like centuries.

"Can you see me?" I whispered cautiously. Afraid of the answer.

"Holy shit. This is too weird," she muttered. Or thought. Or something. Her lips didn't move.

"Can you see me, Eileen?" I asked again. I was surprised by her thought language because I'd never heard her use obscenity in all the time I'd known her.

"What the fuck are you doing in my bedroom, Arthur?"

"This is a dream, Eileen," I said, still stunned by her language.

She sat up. Or at least some part of her sat up. A luminescent part. The rest of her remained in its curled up position. "But I can see you, Arthur. Don't give me that shit. What the fuck are you doing here?"

"Look at yourself," I said, pointing to her recumbent form.

She turned and looked down. "Oh my God. Oh shit. Oh goddamned motherfucking shit!"

"This is a dream," I whispered. Whatever it's called when you lower the volume of a telepathic communication.

She looked at me again. "Did you know you've got a dream woody, Arthur?"

I looked down at myself. My cock, glowing like my hands had, was stiff. I felt embarrassed and vulnerable. I looked at Eileen.

She was looking at my cock.

"I think I've been in love with you since the first time I saw you," I said. I didn't seem to be able to help myself.

"Mmmmmm. I wondered," she said still gazing at my cock. "You always seemed to act kind of strange when I was around."

"Was I that obvious?"

She looked up, into my eyes. "No, you weren't obvious. I was looking for the signs. I've had feelings for you too."

"I think I must be dreaming," I said. We both laughed.

"Shit this is strange," she said. "How did this happen?"

"I've been trying to have lucid dreams, dreams I consciously control, and I seem to have succeeded. Except I didn't know it was possible to make contact with other people. That is if you're really Eileen and not some image created by my imagination."

"I feel like me," she said. "Strange, but like me in a strange fucking situation. Are you my neighbor Arthur? Or are you some demon wearing Arthur as a disguise?"

"As far as I can tell I'm your neighbor Arthur. I don't feel like a demon."

She floated free of her body, which was still fetally curled, and reached out to grasp my cock. "Mmmmm. I've wanted to do this for a long time."

The sensation wasn't anything like physical touching. More akin to energy flowing into energy, throwing off twinkling stars like an Independence Day sparkler. I reached out and touched her breast with the same result.

"Oh shit, this is cool," she said. "I never imagined anything like this was possible in my wildest···"

"Dreams." I said. We laughed again. Then she took my cock in her mouth and the laughter ended precipitously. The nerves, or whatever, in our astral, or whatever, bodies must correspond pretty closely to our physical bodies because feeling her mouth around my cock took me to another planet entirely.

It was at this moment that Hector's alarm clock went off. If we'd been in our physical, or whatever, bodies I think I might very well have lost my penis given the amount of pressure, ethereal as it was, I felt at that moment. Eileen's gossamer self jumped back into her body and disappeared. I remained for only a moment longer, long enough to see Hector reach out to slap the button on the clock, glance at his wife's bare back, and struggle into sitting position at the edge of the bed. Then I too was gone.

The dream, when I awoke, was etched on my consciousness. But, in the full light of day, it didn't seem real. I retrieved the morning paper and glanced over at Eileen's house wondering if she was remembering the same images. I was afraid I'd never know. On the other hand I was shocked by the experience, by the intimacy, so another part of me hoped nothing would change. And I think she felt the same way. The few times our paths crossed in the next couple of days neither of us could look the other in the eye. Then one evening when I got home from work I found Anita and Eileen on the back deck drinking margaritas. At one point, while Anita was in the bathroom, Eileen said very quietly, "I had the strangest dream about you."

My heart started pounding. "I know," I said after a long moment of silence. She looked at me. In the light streaming out of the kitchen window I could see her blush.

"I apologize for my language," she said. "I can't seem control myself in dreams the way I can in real life."

"I wondered about that," I said.

Anita returned and nothing more was said on the subject.

I continued to experiment with my dreams but it was six weeks before I worked up the nerve to visit Eileen again. Anita had organized a BBQ bash at our house and Eileen, Hector, and their two young sons, were invited along with several other neighborhood families. So, on the night before the party, I suppose because she was in my thoughts, I was once again in her bedroom. Her dream body, or whatever it was, popped up the moment I appeared.

"Oh, I was hoping you'd come," she said. Or thought.

"I wasn't sure you'd want me to," I said.

"Oh Arthur. Arthur. I've been longing for you ever since the last time. I've wanted you so much. I've been driving Hector crazy, fucking him every which way I can think of. But shit, it's not the same. I think of how it felt to have your hard dream cock in my mouth and the juice runs down my legs."

A man doesn't get many invitations like this in his life. I reached out to her and our bodies flowed together. It wasn't penetration in the usual sense but rather a combining, a commingling, an interconnecting on the deepest levels, becoming One in a way impossible for physical bodies. We weren't a man and a woman. We were two playful erotic energies joined in a ball of pleasure. We were two children before the age of sexual division frolicking with a marvelous new toy with wholehearted delight. Two puppies wrestling in the grass.

We soon realized that gravity was not a concern. Not long after that we became aware that a shared thought could take us anywhere. We ended up on a Florida beach, hovering like butterflies. Our eyes were wide open, with me feeling her pleasure knowing she was feeling mine.

"Is this how they fuck in heaven?" She asked.

"Do they fuck in heaven?" Was my response.

"Well, fucking is heavenly, isn't it?"

"This is fucking heavenly, yes."

"Are you saying I'm a heavenly fuck? How sweet."

"Fucking A." I grunted.

"Shut up, for heaven's sake, and fuck me." She sighed.

There wasn't the familiar building up to an abrupt orgasmic release but rather a growing intensity, like the turning of a rheostat, that reached a powerful crescendo and then slowly subsided. It was like being immersed in warm honey and then stimulated with the vibrations of a billion angel's wings. It wasn't me feeling it. It was Us feeling it. And sharing that mutual feeling was the deepest pleasure of all. We were One in the profoundest pleasure possible.

"Oh." Eileen exclaimed, once the vibrations had died away. "I've never felt anything like that before."

I was speechless. We were lying naked in the sand under the blazing sun, cuddling together. 2300 miles away Hector's goddamned alarm clock went off and Eileen was jerked out of my arms. Then I too was drawn back.

"You must have had quite a dream," Anita said, leering across the breakfast table. "You splooged all over my butt last night. Or, more precisely, this morning."

I looked at her startled, a shamed little boy welling up inside me, "I'm sorry."

"I'm razzing you, honey. But it better have been me you were dreaming about," she said with an edgy gleam in her eye. I wasn't sure how serious she was.

"Of course it was," I said, lying and knowing she knew I was lying. She just laughed.

Most of the rest of the day was spent preparing for the BBQ. I often found myself recalling the magical time with Eileen and smiling. Not just smiling but humming and walking with a bounce in my step.

"That must have been quite some dream," Anita said again, late in the afternoon, just before the guests were scheduled to arrive. The little boy welled up once more and I wilted. "Hey, honey, I'm teasing you," she said, seeing my distress. "I don't care who it was. I kind of got a kick out of seeing you so excited."

That only made me feel worse.

And then we were caught in the whirlwind of our invited guests arriving. I focused on greeting the men while Anita took care of the women and children. I avoided Eileen but could sense her hurt and bewilderment. Later, after everyone had eaten and the party had settled down to rambling conversation, I went into the bathroom in the master bedroom to take a leak and found Eileen sitting on the bed I shared with Anita when I came out. I stopped cold.

"What's the matter Arthur? You haven't said two words to me."

"I don't like cheating on Anita," I said

"Oh, are we having an affair?"

"Physically, no, but mentally I have to say yes."

"Well, no one I know is a mind reader that I'm aware of so I think we're safe."

"You want to keep doing it?" I asked.

"God yes. Don't you, Arthur? It feels so incredible."

"Yes, it does. But I do feel guilty. I've never cheated on Anita."

"It was a dream. Haven't you had wet dreams before?"

"Yessssss."

"Did you feel guilty?"

"No," I said softly.

"Well, this is the same thing."

"Not exactly. Those other dreams were simply dreams. This is real in a weird kind of way. I mean, we're here in my bedroom talking about a sex dream we had together for God's sake."

"But it was still a dream, nothing more. No one's going to catch us in flagrante delicto. I'm not going to get pregnant."

"I don't know Eileen. I have to think about it."

It hurt to see the look of disappointment on her face. She looked as if she was about to cry. I turned away and for most of the evening my thoughts were in turmoil.

And then I watched my small daughter caught up in playing with her friends, all of them running around the yard, their faces glowing with joy. Like puppies, playing in the grass.

Not long after that I took Anita aside. And told her the whole story. I could tell she didn't believe me, that she thought I was describing a run of the mill wet dream.

"Honey, I'm not jealous of your dreams," she said. "I'm glad you're having fun. But if you touch Eileen in the here and now I will break off your arm and beat you with it. Comprender?"

"Yes, dear."

She gave me a good humored scowl.

"And darling, I'm going to try to meet you in my dreams the way

I did with Eileen." I told her.

"I can't wait," she said, clearly unimpressed. I knew that if I succeeded she might extend the prohibition against touching Eileen into the dream world as well but I'd wait to cross that bridge when it appeared.

One of the traditions of these gatherings was for me to bring out my guitar and accompany a sing-a-long around a fire winking and sparking in the fire pit. And tonight I played for almost three hours before people began to nod off. So, for the last song of the evening I began plunking out the chords of the Huddie Ledbetter classic. I saw a secret happy smile cross Eileen's face as she recognized the words I began to sing. The others heard the standard version but with the simple substitution of a single syllable she and I heard something different.

Eileen goodnight, Eileen goodnight
goodnight Eileen, goodnight Eileen
I'll be with you in my dreams.

"No!" She Said.

"No." She said. "No fucking way. No. No. No. Is there any part of that you don't understand?"

She didn't leave me with many options. I'd just asked my wife of fourteen years if she'd be willing to fulfill a fantasy of mine of seeing her with another man. I knew her well enough to know that this would probably be her first reaction but still her vehemence startled me. I could tell that she was upset and very hurt.

"How could you want such a thing? Why? To see some strange man use me. No. No, fucking, way." Her eyes glistened with tears.

I put my arms around her. She was stiff and distant, her eyes averted. I held her and stroked her back. My desires weren't something I could easily explain. I loved her. I loved her so much. And our sex life wasn't bad although we'd settled into something of a routine. But I had the feeling we were missing a dimension of life and somehow this idea of including another man seemed as if it would open a door to that space beyond. It was a feeling I found impossible to communicate.

We both felt bruised for the next couple of days. And the week or so after that was a mixture of remoteness and quiet flashes of the old intimacy. Finally, as we watched an old movie on TV, the lost warmth returned and she came to lie beside me on the couch. It felt so good to feel her pressing against me, rubbing her bottom against my crotch, and later to feel her kisses grow hot as I touched her soft smooth skin and her slick wetness, to hear her sighing as I slipped inside.

Yet that small grain of irritating sand that I'd brought into our relationship remained. For me it was a matter of struggling to understand what it was I wanted, what it was I felt was missing.

For Adele, my wife, as I learned later, the experience was one of opening a place in her mind that had been, until I'd given her a key, padlocked with fear and the strictures of convention.

At the time we each felt alone. We could share sweet warmth within the confines of the old assumptions but as we explored further, roaming among the possibilities of love outside the norm, the air grew more frigid. But, as we subsequently discovered, we each, in our own way, found the adventure bracing.

For a long time I couldn't get past the images of seeing Adele opening wide and a stranger's cock invading her. She'd, to the best of my knowledge, and I believed her, only known two other men before me. Two short term affairs before we'd met. So I thought it was the invasion, the taboo, that stirred me. In my imagination I heard her quiet cries, stranger's names spoken with ardor, but didn't listen with care.

Unbeknownst to me, while I was at work and before the kids came home from school, Adele had begun searching the Internet for ways to use this little key I'd given her, ways to assuage the irritation of the grain of sand. Seek and ye shall find, we're told. Seeking on the Internet can go a long long way. No telling what you'll find. One of the doors that opened for Adele was a site that offered a smorgasbord of people with a jaw dropping variety of sexual interests. Very timidly, after going back to the site again and again, she decided to place a little profile about herself. One not entirely true. She was not in the least bit prepared for the onslaught.

The first day after placing her profile there were twenty two messages from men. The day after that there were thirty four. Plus four from women. It got worse after that. At first it was kind of interesting to look at a strange penis but once she'd seen about thirty five the novelty sort of wore off. She began looking for something a little more distinctive. Most of the messages were short and not very illuminating. From time to time a man would send a clothed photo. Once in a very great while a man would send a clothed photo and a message that appeared to have been written by a thinking person. These were the ones she decided to answer. The first order of business being to straighten out all the crooked parts in her profile.

One of the first men she connected with was a man named Rob who lived about two hours away. Far enough not to be an immediate threat but close enough to be available. She soon learned that Rob had some knowledge about the kind of situation I, her husband, was proposing.

"Why?" she wailed, via email. "Why would he want me to fuck some stranger?"

"Who do *you* want to fuck?" was his reply.

That brought her to a standstill. She worked through the gamut of responses. It took her four days to get back to him. "I'm happy with Greg (he's my husband). I love fucking him. The sex has gotten kind of same o' same o', I'll admit, but he's still my main man."

"Why'd you place the ad then?" Rob asked. "If you're happy that's fine. I'm delighted for you. But I can't help but feel that there's more to this than that. I've done group sex, I've been in threesomes, and I know that women can get into these things just as much as men. You say that you're happy with Greg, and as far as I can tell you are, but I get the sense that you're hoping there's something more."

It took seven days for her to get back to him. "I apologize for taking so long to write. You gave me a lot to think about in your last email. It hasn't been easy for me these last few days. When you talk about group sex and threesomes I have to tell you, even though I've known you for so short a time, it makes me wet. I feel so nasty telling you that. But I think you're right that I'm looking for something. Greg has no idea. You know, when he first told me he'd like to see me with other men it made me feel all shriveled up inside. As if I wasn't good enough or something. But when I started writing you I began to think, This could be my experience; I could have fun with this. And it made the whole thing feel different."

"Of course it's your experience, sweetie," Rob replied. "You're the one creating this, not Greg. He may have gotten the balls rolling, so to speak, but you're the one who placed an ad. You're the one who asked the questions. You're the one who got wet when I started talking about threesomes and moresomes. And I'm here if you need me. I don't need any particular thing to happen. I'm trying to help you discover what it is you want."

As I said, this colloquy, for the most part, was occurring at times when I wasn't present. And, to be quite frank, I wasn't aware of the effect they were having on Adele for some time. She was more responsive, yes, and we made love more frequently. But, with a solemn bow to the male ego, I assumed she was finding me somehow more stimulating. Little did I know that Rob was the midhusband (as opposed to midwife) of my marital pleasures. But even a head as thick as mine has to absorb a few shafts of light eventually.

I began to realize that Adele was much more involved in using the computer than she'd used to be. Checking email before we went to bed, rising early to be the first one on. When I asked her about it she said it was some new game she'd found or an email she expected from a friend. For awhile this made sense to me but I slowly became aware of the fact that the urgency with which she approached the keyboard outweighed the ostensible purpose. And then, one afternoon, while Adele and the kids were at the mall, I explored the system until I found Rob's emails and email address. It wasn't all that hard, since Adele was not in the hacker class of computer user.

The following Monday I sent him an email from my office computer informing him of my discovery. His reply was terse and to the point.

"Hi Greg, it doesn't surprise me that you broke the code. There probably wasn't one. But I'm her friend, not yours. At least not yet. And I won't betray her confidence, if there's any confidence left to betray after your snooping. --Rob"

I wrote Rob back to tell him that I loved Adele with all my heart and that I had no wish to hurt her. I told him that the main reason I'd contacted him was to open a dialogue with someone who obviously meant a lot to her.

He wrote back to say that he thought it should be Adele's choice to decide whether he and I opened a dialogue.

To tell you the truth this guy was getting on my nerves.

Assuming it was very likely Rob, testy as he was, would tell Adele I'd found her out, I decided that the best course was to talk to my wife myself.

"You WHAT? You sonofabitch. Those were my private fucking emails goddamn it. You had no goddamn right. Yougoddamn-motherfuckingsonofabitch." were her exact words. A string of words I'd almost never heard her use. Clearly she was more angry than usual.

"Adele, sweetheart. Adele." I tried to speak softly. "Honey, I'm not trying to put you on the spot. But I'm your husband, Greg, remember Greg, and I'd like to know what's going on. I liked what this Rob guy said to you even though I'm not crazy about what he said to me."

"This Rob guy, huh," she said, "this Rob guy fucking understands me. Which is more than I can say for you."

I took a deep breath and told myself that she was coming from an emotional place that wasn't connected to an adult perspective. I wasn't at all certain I was connected to that particular perspective either. "Honey, I love you. I want to understand. I'd like for both of us to be able to talk to Rob and find out if he can help us see this differently. He seems to have the experience that we don't have."

After several long moments of glaring, the Adele I knew began to peek out of that angry face. "You aren't pissed at me for going behind your back?" She asked.

"Honey bunch, this has been a tough time for both of us. I think there's a lot we haven't shared with each other. That's as true of me as it is of you. We've both gone behind the other's back." Once I'd said that it was as if the ice had thawed. She flowed into my arms. We spent most of the night sharing the highlights of our individual explorations. Finally, as we talked, I realized that what I wanted was for her to be free to explore her deepest desires, sexual or otherwise. My image of her opening her legs to a strange man was a metaphor for her opening herself to her truest potentials.

She, on the other hand, felt a strong personal connection with Rob that didn't have anything to do with abstract conceptual metaphors of abstruse meaning. She liked this guy. He turned her on. This was frightening for me and I told her so. In my fantasies the man involved had always been a stranger we had chanced to meet; someone we'd never see again. The way she was talking, Rob might be a part of our lives, in and out of bed, for some time to come. And that brought up some deeply buried insecurities in me. I was afraid I'd be found inadequate when compared with him.

"What? You want to back out of this?" She asked, with more than a hint of anger.

"No, hon," I said, "I'm aware that I started all this and I will follow through. I simply want you to know what I'm feeling. That I'm realizing that things happen differently in reality than in my fantasies. And it scares me sometimes."

She snuggled up against me and placed my hand on her warm breast. "I understand, sweetheart; I get scared too. I love you Greg. Don't ever forget that. And I'm glad we're sharing this adventure together."

"I love you too," I said, lifting her leg to slide into her from behind. "God honey, you are so hot and wet."

"Hmmmm," was her response.

The next morning, after the kids had left the house on their usual Saturday visits to friends, we both sat down to write Rob an email summing up our late night conversation. Early in the evening he emailed his reply.

"Hi Adele and Greg, I was delighted to hear that the two of you

12

have talked things out and that I'm still in the picture. I was very uncomfortable with the way things were. And Greg, I apologize for being so hard on you before." He went on to describe some of his experiences with other couples and how they'd worked out. His tone was very matter of fact and both Adele and I felt reassured by his obvious knowledge of the subject. We agreed that he seemed to be a thoughtful and caring person.

Another result was that we both became very aroused. I had to smile as I watched Adele wiggle in her chair as she read the words on the screen, her mouth slightly open and her tongue running across her lips now and then. I had a stiff one that caused me to do some wiggling of my own. If the kids hadn't been around I think we both would have started masturbating. As it was the kids got hustled off to bed at the stroke of nine and Adele and I raced for our bedroom slinging clothes left and right. Our love making that night was anything but routine. The fevered passion we'd thought we'd lost burned as brightly as it ever had.

One of Rob's stories involved a woman who liked to have him come on her tongue. At the moment Adele felt my climax approaching she hissed, "My tongue, baby, do it on my tongue." We'd never done this before. She'd always made negative comments about the come shots we'd seen in porn videos. And here she was begging for one. I pulled out of her cunt and straddled her chest, vigorously stroking my cock. Our eyes locked and she stuck out her tongue. I'd never seen her so aroused. With a loud groan I spilled my pearls into her pink mouth. She held her mouth open until the last drop fell. "Kiss me." She cried. I leaned down and tasted myself as our tongues wrestled.

That was the first of many new things we added to our erotic repertoire. Over the next few weeks we corresponded with Rob. He very patiently answered our questions and shared more of his knowledge. We also began to exchange phone calls; Adele talking with him most of the time. Then Adele and I decided we were ready to take the plunge. Adele phoned Rob to give him the good news and we began to make plans.

At last the big day arrived. We dropped the kids off at Adele's mother's house and made the two hour drive to Rob's home town. Both of us getting more and more nervous as we got closer. We rented a room at the motel that Rob had recommended and walked to the restaurant where we'd agreed to meet. We held hands tightly, like two children walking through a dark forest. A tall, slim, man with long hair rose from the bench when we walked in and met us halfway. He had a warm smile and a calm demeanor that helped us begin to feel a little more at ease.

"You must be Greg and Adele," he said in a resonant voice. When we nodded he leaned down to kiss Adele on the cheek and then shook my hand. Adele preceded us to the table and I noticed that Rob checked out her legs and bottom. He caught my eye while we were seating ourselves and somehow I knew that he was aware that I'd seen him looking. He showed no sign of embarrassment. I also got the impression that he'd liked what he saw.

At first the conversation was a little stilted but Rob kept asking us questions and sharing his thoughts and soon we were all talking as if we'd known one another for years. Rob and Adele especially. I think if he'd been any other man I would have felt threatened but in some way I didn't understand he created an ambiance in which those feelings never even began.

In part, I think, it was due to what he called his 'one ground rule' that he'd shared with us in an early email. He'd said that if any one of us was uncomfortable about what was happening we could say 'Stop'. He guaranteed that he'd stop even if no one else did. It gave me a much needed sense of control.

Once we'd finished eating and established that we all did indeed want to go through with this the three of us walked back to the motel. Adele and I were holding hands again but now it was more from anticipation than from fear. Rob wore a small sweet smile. There was another moment of awkwardness when we closed the door behind us but Rob broke through that by unbuttoning his shirt and saying, "Let's get naked." And, in no time, we were.

Neither Rob or I were hard at this juncture. Adele sat down on the edge of the bed, her breasts swaying, and beckoned us over. "Oh boy." She said as she took our soft cocks in her hands, "Every girl's dream." She took Rob's cock in her mouth first.

"Unless the girl's lesbian," Rob said with a laugh. "Oh yeah, that feels good." I could see him start to grow hard. I felt myself growing hard too. Soon Adele had her hands full. She pulled us together and took the heads of both our cocks into her mouth, looking up at us. I could see that Rob was about the same length as I but a bit thicker.

"God," Adele whispered, pulling away from us, "this makes me feel like a slut."

Rob had a slight frown, "you know I don't like that word. You have every right to be a sexual person."

"Oh, take the stick out of your ass," Adele said, "I feel like a slut and I like it."

Rob laughed, "Okay, okay."

"Quit the yakking and suck, slut," I said.

Rob began fingering her pussy while I played with her tits. I found it strange how normal this all felt. Here Adele and I were butt naked with a guy we'd only met a few hours ago and we're making silly jokes. Adele fell back on the bed and spread her legs. Rob and I both looked at her in awe. She was drinking it in. She grabbed her knees and opened herself wide.

"One of you schmucks gonna fuck me or do I have to grab some kid off the street?" Adele asked forcefully. Rob and I looked at each other and then I gave him the 'you first' gesture with my right hand. A second later I was watching him enter my wife. My fantasy, voiced so many months ago, had come true. I'd given her the key and she'd unlocked the door. "Oh Rob, that feels so good," she sighed. I knelt beside the bed, leaning on it, as I watched her. She looked so beautiful to me, her chest flushed with arousal.

Rob looked at me, a hint of concern in his eyes. "Go man," I said, "Fuck that slut. Make that hot cunted bitch cum." Adele turned to me, her eyes glowing, a big smile on her lips. And Rob did as he was told.

And then it was my turn. And, after a period of talk and resting, his again. He lay down on his back and Adele straddled him, holding his cock so she could guide him into herself. Once he was inside she lay on his chest as he held her.

"Ever try a dp?" I heard him ask her. She pushed herself up on her arms.

"What's a dp?"

"Double penetration," I said. "Two cocks inside you." I felt myself and knew I was hard enough.

"How the fuck would I try a dp if this is the first time I've been with two guys?" She retorted.

"Oh yeah, I forgot," Rob said. "Well?"

Adele looked at me. I shrugged and looked down at my cock. Adele looked down at my cock. Rob was looking at my cock too.

"Sure, why not," Adele said.

I climbed up between Rob's legs and positioned myself. Slowly I slid my cock into Adele's pussy, feeling Rob's cock beneath mine.

"Oh God." Adele said, her voice saturated with lust, excitement, and wonderment. "I feel so full. Oh, this is wild."

"Do you want us to stop?" I asked, giving Rob a devilish grin over Adele's shoulder.

"No." she moaned. "No fucking way. God no. No. No."

"Could you repeat that?" I chortled. "I thought I heard a part I didn't understand."

Balls of Cobalt Blue

"I'll give you fifty dollars if you'll skinny dip in the fountain right now," Penny said as she parked her bike beside mine in the little alley next to the restaurant.

Vicente, our employer at El Rojo Gallo, had assigned me the task of scrubbing the ring of scum off the colorful Mexican tiles that lined the reservoir. Because I'm a guy, I guess. None of the women had to do these kinds of chores even though, as a waiter, my status was the same as theirs.

"Given my money situation I might take you up on that," I said, turning to look at her. The brush dangled in my hand. She flashed me a roguish grin and disappeared through the front door. I sat savoring the after image of her vigorous stocky body fading into the interior. Remembering the sparkle in her eyes.

It was the end of the tourist season and things were slow. Which was part of the reason I was out here scrubbing the fountain. I thought about Penny's challenge as I went back to work. It made the morning sun brighter, the air piquant.

Four days ago we'd urged a sluggish afternoon along with episodic conversation and Penny had mentioned that she'd been an English major at Iowa State University. Although I'd always found her attractive it was at that point that my interest in her quickened. Once she'd returned from checking on one of her tables I told her I was a writer. Her eyes filled with new respect. I told her I'd posted a number of my poems and one of my short stories online. One of my tables required attention. When I got back she asked me how she could access my writing. With a bit of trepidation, having had a couple of bad experiences mixing my private passion with the politics of the workplace, I gave her the Internet address.

"You're a very good writer, Stephen," she said the first time she saw me the next morning. "I'm impressed. I liked your short story a lot. Do you have any more?"

This is where things got sticky for me. "Yes, I do, but I'm not sure I feel comfortable sharing them with you." I could see that all I'd succeeded in doing was grab her attention.

"Why not?"

"Well," I said, "they're dirty. Erotica, if you will."

She gave me a speculative look and then laughed. "Stephen. I'm thirty-six years old, not a child. And whatever your fantasies are it's all basic human stuff."

"I'm not concerned about you so much as the fact that we work together. I've gotten into some difficulties at other jobs when I shared this side of myself."

Throughout the day she kept pleading her case. "I enjoy hardcore porn sometimes," she whispered once, picking up a coffee pot as I was returning one. "Believe me, I'm unshockable," she added later when our paths crossed again, "I'd love to see those stories."

I was amused by her attempts to convince me how worldly she was, how dirty minded. Yet her persistence made me feel shy and on the spot. But at last, flattered by her insistence, I gave her the Internet address. The next day, Wednesday, was her usual day off so this morning was the first time I'd seen her since giving her the key to my secret fantasy life. And the first words out of her mouth involved asking me to take off my clothes. I assumed she'd liked what she'd read.

"Hey," I said when I saw her after I'd finished cleaning the fountain. "You're no fun. You didn't stay to watch."

"You can always do an encore."

I mumbled something. On one hand I was shaken by her flirtatious challenges but on the other I enjoyed them very much. I liked the direction things were going. There were several more brief exchanges, all in a light teasing tone, in which we both kept upping the ante. And then the noon rush came and we didn't have the privacy or the time for more words. But my brain was churning. This was so much fun. I loved the fact that she wasn't backing down. I decided to confront her with a proposal.

"Let's go outside," I said, once the rush was over. She gave me a quizzical glance but didn't offer any resistance. We left Brooke and Cindy to watch our stations. "I've been thinking about our conversation," I said. We passed through the side door into the alley. "Usually I take women out of their comfort zones but you've

17

taken me out of mine."

"I'm sorry, Stephen," she said.

"Oh no," I said. "I like it. But I have a dare for you."

"Okay," she said.

"The fountain out front doesn't work for me because I'd just as soon keep my job but how about if we could find someplace outdoors reasonably private?"

"And?"

"And you can keep your fifty dollars. If you show me yours I'll show you mine."

"Okay," she said. Without the least bit of hesitation. I was more than a little stunned. At this point Vicente's brown face appeared on the other side of the screen door and informed us that we had customers. Penny and I gazed into each other's eyes for a long moment and then I pulled the door open and we walked inside.

And I started to sweat. Bullets. I took orders and delivered plates of burritos and enchiladas but my mind was clenched with fear. What if she goes to Vicente and says, "Stephen asked me to get naked and I'm very offended." What if she thinks I'm nuts and closes down. What if. What if. I was hoping for the best but prepared for the worst. I caught her eye a couple of times and tried to gauge her state of mind but couldn't. Things slowed down again and I decided to confront the issue directly. I stopped her outside the door of the women's restroom.

"Was I out of line?" I said. Our eyes met.

"Concerning our conversation earlier? About someplace outdoors?"

"Yeah."

She shrugged in a way that conveyed to me that she didn't have a problem.

"You're cool with it?" I asked.

"Sure," she said. "I don't agree to things I don't feel right about." I was giddy with relief.

Later, during the quiet afternoon, we went on to plan the details of when and where. We decided on Saturday afternoon after work, since the next day, Friday, she had an appointment. We agreed that we'd ride our bikes to a place she knew of not far from a house where she used to live.

"I'm used to women either closing down or running away when I come up with these harebrained ideas," I said. "It means a lot to me that you're willing to do this."

"Life's too short to let your fears limit you," she told me. "And anyway, I grew up with four brothers so I don't find men to be especially scary."

"I used to go to the nude beach when I lived in California. I've been to a couple of nudist camps too. So I've had some experience with this sort of thing."

"I've done a few things like that myself," she said. "Taking showers outdoors while camping with friends. Skinny dipping. I'm comfortable with my body so it's no big deal."

SHE PUT IN A SHORT day on Friday, before leaving for her appointment, but I had a chance to talk with her for a few minutes and didn't see any signs that she was having reservations.

On Saturday morning, before going to work, I rolled up a thick blanket and attached it to my bike with bungee cords. I also put a couple of condoms in my wallet. Neither of us had broached the subject of our being sexual together but then nothing we'd said took it out of consideration. My nerves sang with anticipation as I pedaled to the restaurant.

She was parking her bike as I rode up and I could see that she'd caught sight of the blanket. We exchanged a quick secret smile before she headed inside. I wasn't far behind.

The time dragged by. We chatted when we had the chance but neither of us mentioned the adventure we'd planned. At long last it was time for us to leave and we walked out to our bikes together. Since she knew where we were going she took the lead once we'd mounted up. I followed her for a couple of miles until she stopped at the beginning of a gravel road that led down into a rocky canyon. On the floor of the canyon two sets of railroad tracks ran parallel to the primitive road.

"We'll have to walk the bikes from here," she said. It took some effort to get the bikes down the steep decline but soon the road became relatively level.

"So, what got you started writing erotic stories?"

"Well," I said, "sex can drag us into situations where we learn things about ourselves that we might not be motivated to discover any other way. That interests me."

She nodded.

"We enter into something thinking that all we want is an orgasm and emerge with a new way of perceiving the world."

"Sounds serious," she said. She was walking enough in front of me that I couldn't see her face but I could hear her smile.

"Yeah, well, to be quite frank I started out writing stories about what I call 'passionate plumbing'. Detailed descriptions of sex acts, that is. But somewhere along the line the sex acts became less interesting to me than the dynamics between the people involved."

"Hmmm," she said.

Several minutes later we were climbing high into the rocks beside the road. When we got to a reasonably flat area behind several large boulders I spread out the blanket I'd taken off my bike. We both hesitated for a second, now that the moment of truth had arrived, and then I pulled my t-shirt over my head. I looked over and saw that she'd kicked off her sandals and was sliding her spandex shorts from under her dress.

"You know, I didn't wear a dress until I was twenty-three," she said. "The only reason I wear them now is because Vicente insists we do."

While I untied my shoes she slipped out of her dress, standing there in a pair of lime-green v-string panties and a multi-colored bathing suit top. I unbuckled my belt, unzipped, and pushed my jeans down my legs.

"We've wondered if you wore underwear. Brooke and I said you didn't and Cindy said you did."

"I haven't worn underwear since I was a kid," I said. "Didn't make sense to me."

She unhooked the top and let her medium sized breasts swing free. Tucking her fingers into the sides of her panties she pushed them down. I noted that she was almost hairless, though not shaven.

"You're so white." She said. "Your arms and face are tanned but the rest of you isn't."

"At the nudist camp they called people like me 'cottontails'."

"Well, I'll never have that problem," she said, smiling as she sat down beside me.

I lay on my side, leaning on my elbow, and drank in the sight of her body as she stretched out on her back. Her nipples were the size of thimbles and almost as dark as blackberries. She was, what my fourth grade teacher called, 'pleasantly plump'. Very pleasantly.

She observed my gaze. "I feel I need to say something," she said. "I realize that my agreeing to get naked with you might suggest otherwise but I don't do casual sex."

I was disappointed. I couldn't help it. But to be fair to her I had to admit that she'd never hinted that sex would be part of the experience. "You don't care if I get blue balls?" I said, keeping my tone light.

"Not really," she said with that sparkle in her eyes. We both laughed.

"I haven't been with anyone for awhile," I said, my voice more emotional than I'd intended.

"Yeah, for me too."

"What do you do for sex? Or doesn't it bother you?"

She turned her head to look at me directly. "I'm not sure what you mean by 'bother'. But I masturbate." I nodded and she turned away. We could hear a train approaching.

The train rumbled past. I wondered if the engineer could see us. Maybe our faces. I thought our bodies were probably hidden by the rocks.

"Perhaps we could masturbate together," I said. "We'd be sharing what we do separately. Not exactly like having sex but there is intimacy. And stimulation."

She thought about that for awhile. "I could see doing that," she said. "But not today."

The conversation rambled on into more ordinary topics. We talked about work and shared a bit about our pasts. She seemed to feel comfortable with me. I felt a deep gratitude to her for giving me the gift of her nakedness. Another train passed, going the other way.

"I'd better be getting back," she said at last.

We put our clothes back on, rolled up the blanket, and climbed down out of the rocks. Recovering our bikes we walked back up the gravel road, chatting as we went, until we reached the street.

"This was fun," she said. We stood side by side.

"For me too," I said. "How about having dinner with me tomorrow? At my place."

"As long as we're clear about the sex thing," she said, giving me a meaningful glance.

"Of course, Penny. I like you. I plain enjoy being with you. Would hamburgers and a salad be too prosaic?"

"Sounds good."

We climbed onto our bikes and headed in opposite directions.

"Thank you," she called as she crossed the street.

"No, thank *you*," I called back. I was rewarded with another sparkle from her dark eyes. It warmed me to my core.

I GOT TO WORK before she did the next morning and was wrapping silverware in napkins with Cindy and Brooke when she arrived.

"I hope that little problem with the color blue got worked out," she said. Brooke and Cindy looked mystified. Penny and I shared a secret smile.

"No, but that's okay," I said.

The day passed quickly. The restaurant was busy as it often is on Sundays when the locals either decide to let someone else do the cooking or stop by for something after church. Once our shift was over I gave her directions to my house. She agreed to come by around five.

I spent the rest of the afternoon tidying things up and readying the outdoor grill. My activity made my two cats, Harold and Maude, nervous and they kept chasing each other around the house until I cranked up the vacuum cleaner which sent them both scurrying under the bed.

I heard the crunch of gravel in my driveway just before five and opened the door to investigate. Penny had stepped out of a firetruck-red Jeep Wrangler and was reaching back inside.

"I didn't know you had a car," I said. "All I've seen you ride is the bike."

"Yes, well, I like to ride the bike. I need the exercise. And gas prices being what they are, you know. I hope you don't mind if I brought dessert," she said, holding a box containing a pie in her hands.

"No, that's great. I didn't think of dessert." I stepped aside to let her in.

"Oh, wow." She said, looking around my living room at the profusion of books. "You could open a library."

"I can't seem to pass a used book store without buying a couple," I said, leading her into the kitchen. "And I find it very hard to part with one once it's bought." Harold and Maude had appeared, tails in the air, to examine the guest and give her their stamp of approval. "These are my cats," I said, introducing them. "I hope you're not allergic, I should have asked."

"I love cats. These two are quite a pair." After depositing the pie on the counter she crouched down to get better acquainted. Her t-shirt fell away from her body and I could see she was wearing a regular bra this time. Turquoise.

I picked up the plate on which four hamburger patties had been thawing. "I'll get these on the grill and then come back to make the dressing for the salad."

When I returned she was looking through my books. "Very interesting," she said. I mixed the ingredients of the dressing while she continued to browse. Fifteen minutes later everything was ready. We stood next to each other at the counter, built our hamburgers, and filled our salad bowls. And then we carried them outside to the table on the patio. The grill was still exuding flavorful smoke. "Hey, it's nice out here," she said.

We ate in silence, exchanging occasional friendly glances. It felt good to be with her.

"I don't feel ready for pie yet," I said when I finished.

"I don't either."

"But what I would like to do, if you're interested, is listen to A Prairie Home Companion, Garrison Keillor's radio variety show on NPR."

"I'm not familiar with it," she said. "But sure, if you want to."

"They sometimes do skits about English majors I thought you'd enjoy."

"Okay."

"I do have to warn you, though, that about the only comfortable place in the house is my bed. I'm more into buying books than couches or chairs."

Her look and head shake expressed wry amazement. "I guess that's all right. You didn't jump me when you had me naked so I guess I can trust you not to do it now."

We took the dirty dishes into the kitchen. While she made a side trip to the bathroom I turned on the radio and got into the bed next to the wall, arranging the pillows so that we'd be able to sit up. The toilet flushed and a moment later she joined me.

I was gratified to see that she enjoyed the music and humor. They didn't perform a skit about English majors but there were plenty of good laughs without one. About halfway through the program I put my arm around her shoulders. She went kind of still for a couple of minutes and then she relaxed against me, putting her arm on my stomach.

"I liked that," she said when the show ended. "I'll have to start listening." A program of Celtic music began. We continued to lean together without speaking.

"Would you like to get naked with me?" She said at last.

I felt a warm flush spread through my body. "I thought about it but I wasn't going to ask," I said. "I'd love to. I love looking at you."

"I don't know why I like it. I've never done this with anyone else," she said. She got out of bed. I watched as her t-shirt slid up her back and over her head and then was tossed into the upholstered armchair nearby. "I feel comfortable with you somehow," she said, turning to face me as she reached around to unhook her bra. "You have a nice way of looking at me."

I absorbed the revelation of her breasts as the bra joined the t-shirt on the chair. I'd taken off my own t-shirt and was pushing my jeans down my legs. She observed me closely.

"And I like to look too," she said, with a touch of shyness. She unzipped her jeans and pulled them off one leg and then the other. For a moment she stood there wearing only a pair of turquoise v-string panties and then the panties lay on top of the rest of her clothes and she was kneeling on the bed, her breasts swaying, looking at my crotch. "They don't look blue," she said.

We both laughed. The radio was filling the air with the sound of a mournful ballad about some act of violence in an ancient time.

She cupped them. I looked down to see my scrotum nestled in the palm of her small brown hand. She moved her fingers, watching the egg shaped forms shift in their sack. I was beginning to swell. She watched that too.

"Penny," I said. I was having trouble with my breathing. "This isn't quite fair. You're the one who doesn't want us to be sexual."

"I like holding them," she said. "They're definitely not blue, though."

"They will be if you keep this up."

She laughed. She let them go and ran a finger down the ridge of my cock. In an instant I was erect. "You said something about our masturbating together."

"Yeah, I did. If you want to. But what's most important to me is our friendship. I don't want to do anything that's going to jeopardize that."

A shadow crossed her face and her eyes went blank. I didn't understand what was happening. She sat back on her heels.

"Penny?"

"How do you want to do this?" She asked. Her voice sounded dull. "Side by side?"

"I was thinking you could lie on the bed and I'd sit in the chair, facing you," I said. I was struggling to maintain my equilibrium. Something was going on with her and I didn't know what or why.

"Okay, let's do it.'"

I moved slowly. The music on the radio fit the mood. I felt a heaviness of spirit. I climbed off the bed and went to turn off the radio and get a towel. When I returned Penny was lying on the bed with her legs straight out in front of her. She seemed to be staring at her belly button. I picked up her clothes from the chair and put them on my dresser. Then I moved the chair to the foot of the bed. I laid the towel out between Penny's calves and the bed's edge. I was soft.

"We're going to have to do something about the atmosphere here," I said. "I fear it's not conducive to generating orgasms."

Penny looked up, with a rueful laugh. "Yeah, sorry about that. I went off on an emotional tangent." She pulled up her knees, spread her legs slightly, and slid her hand down between them.

From my vantage point I could see her knuckles bobbing but not much more. I played with myself. The idea was enough. I was swelling again.

"Ah," she sighed. I liked hearing the sound her pleasure. Her legs opened wider.

"I guess something feels good over there," I said.

"Yeah," she smiled.

"I'm feeling pretty good over here too."

She looked to where my hand was stroking up and down. "Mmmmm," she said.

I got up, opened the drawer of my nightstand, and fished out a small plastic bottle of lubricant. Sitting down I squeezed a few drops into my palm. "Oh yeah." I said. My hand moved with smooth slickness. Up and down. Penny watched me.

And opened her legs completely. "I don't know about you but I think I'm on the way to generating an orgasm," she said. She closed her eyes and her hips lifted a little. She was pinching her thick nipples with her left hand. Pulling them.

I could see her fingers moving between her puffy outer lips. Not much more. "Oh yeah, me too." In fact I was very close and was careful to keep backing off. "I'd love to see you better," I said. I was having that breathing problem again.

Without opening her eyes she crabbed herself over. I could see everything. Now I could hear the squishy sounds of her wetness as her fingers played.

"Oh God Penny. Thank you. That's beautiful." I squeezed out a couple of more drops of lubricant onto my palm and stroked myself. "I'm close. Would you like to see me come?"

She opened her eyes and sat up part way, supporting herself on her left elbow. Her right hand kept busy. I knelt against the bed where I'd put the towel. I drank in the sight of her.

"Oh yeah, this is for you, honey. Oh yeah. Oh yeah." I could feel it coming. I stroked myself faster. I looked at her face. She was watching me avidly. "Here it comes." Her eyes locked on mine for an instant and then dropped down again. Pearly spurts shot out across the towel.

She fell back as if she'd been struck, eyes closed. Her left hand slipped from underneath her bottom and the fingers found her opening. The sounds of squishiness were quite loud now. "Oh, oh, oh, oh," she was saying with soft puffs of breath. Then she clenched. And quivered. And relaxed. Slowly she rolled over on her side and curled into a fetal position. Jerking slightly from time to time.

I looked down at her full rounded body. Still stroking myself. Still half hard.

Minutes passed.

"Wow," she said, turning over on her back. "That was a good idea you had. I haven't come like that for awhile."

"It was good for me too," I said. "Thank you."

"I've never seen a man shoot like that before. They've always done it inside me. I liked seeing it come out. And to hear the sounds you made."

I sat back in the chair, still holding myself. "I'm glad you enjoyed it."

We were quiet for a long time, lost in our own thoughts. At last Penny stirred and caught sight of the clock on my nightstand.

"I've got to be going," she said. She got off the bed, touching my hair with her left hand as she passed, and went to the dresser where I'd put her clothes. I could hear her getting dressed behind me. "Any big plans for tomorrow?" She asked, coming up beside me.

I hesitated.

"No, wait, I'm sorry," she said. "I just remembered I've got some things to do. I guess we'll see how it goes."

"We'll get together when we get together," I said. I put on my jeans and walked her to the door. I leaned down to give her a kiss but stopped when I saw the closed look on her face. "Goodnight."

"Goodnight Stephen. It was fun. Thank you." She turned to walk out the door and down the sidewalk to her car.

"No, thank *you*," I said. Her laughter floated back to me.

After waving blindly into the headlights of the departing Jeep I closed the door. I was feeling an uneasiness, an uncertainty, that didn't seem to have any logical cause. It had been a satisfying evening. The images flowed through my mind. But there was a disturbing undercurrent like the minor chords in one of those old ballads.

WHEN I GOT TO WORK on Monday Vicente told me she'd taken three days off and wouldn't be in until Thursday. I didn't know what to think. I kept expecting her to show up at the restaurant. But she never did. I didn't know her phone number or address so I couldn't contact her. I didn't even know her last name.

After work, feeling empty and restless, I rode around town on my bike with the half-formed thought of seeing her by chance. I cruised down one street and up another and pondered the mystery of why I felt so drawn to her. Was it that I was so lonely that any woman willing to be with me would have the same effect? But when I thought about the sparkle in her eyes, the intelligence and humor, I doubted that that was the case.

I knew I wasn't in love with her. But I loved being with her. Perhaps, given time, this liking would be transmuted into a romantic love. Perhaps not. What mattered to me was the joy I felt when I caught a glimpse of the gleam in her eyes that could create an epiphanic instant of deep communication between us.

I knew I didn't know her. What Penny felt was another mystery. I did have the sense that I didn't mean as much to her as she meant to me.

She was a strange combination of warmth and elusiveness. I responded to the warmth and was intrigued by the elusiveness. I could think of reasons why she might be so volatile but had no way to confirm whether or not any of my theories had any basis in reality.

Tuesday and Wednesday passed in much the same way. I'd catch myself talking to her in my mind and feel foolish. But I couldn't stop.

WHEN I SAW HER on Thursday morning it was like sunlight breaking through after a gloomy week of rain.

"I was sick," she told me. "I'm feeling a lot better now. Some kind of flu, I guess."

We exchanged glances. The intimate knowledge of our little wild times sparked between us. She smiled.

"Maybe we could hang out together after work?" I said.

She hesitated for a second.

"Go to the park, perhaps?"

"Okay," she said.

It felt so good to be near her again. Watching her move. Catching her eye. Bantering back and forth. In no time at all, it seemed, we were astride our bikes, heading for the park.

"Did you miss me?" She asked lightly. We pedaled side by side along a wide sidewalk.

"Oh Penny." I said. "I can't tell you how much."

She looked at me. I could see that she was taken aback by my intensity.

"They're so blue they could be used to define 'navy blue'," I said, trying to dispel the sudden tension.

She laughed. "That I've got to see. You wouldn't be exaggerating, would you?"

"Maybe a little. I'm sure a viewing could be arranged."

The park was quiet with a single jogger, arms pumping, making the rounds of the track that circled the perimeter and a couple of teenagers tussling in the shade of one of the large trees. We chained our bikes to the low fence that bordered the parking lot and walked across the grass to another tree. I thought about taking her hand but didn't. We sat down a couple of feet apart.

"I like you Penny. I like being with you," I said.

A haunted look clouded her eyes. "I like you too Stephen."

"Last Sunday meant a lot to me. Not just because of what we did. I like your spirit of adventure."

She smiled, gazing up into the tree. "Yeah, that was fun. Kind of crazy, but fun." She lay back, her hands under her head, and turned to look up at me. "Have you done anything like that before?"

"A couple of times."

"It was the first time for me. Most of the guys I've been with haven't been very creative."

"That's too bad," I said, edging closer.

Her eyes followed my movements closely. "Yeah, well, I haven't had much luck with relationships. I've always ended up feeling like I've been put in a cage. They always wanted me to be someone I didn't want to be."

"Not all guys are like that," I said. I was beginning to lean.

"All the guys I've met."

"Maybe," I said, gaining momentum.

"Are you going to kiss me?"

"Yes."

Her lips were soft and sweet but without response. Yet she didn't push me away. I put one hand behind her head, running my fingers into her hair, and draped my other arm across her broad belly. I rubbed my lips against hers, delighting in the softness. I traced the smooth contours with my tongue. She put her hand on my arm. Her mouth opened slightly. I explored the opening. I felt a rush of heat the moment the tip of her tongue tentatively touched mine. And then she was burning. We both were. Our mouths opened wide. We sought to taste each other as fully as possible. My hand covered her breast and she moaned. Time lost its meaning for awhile.

"Oh God," she said, pulling away, gasping. "This is probably a mistake but would you like to come to my place? It isn't far from here." I could clearly read the implication in her eyes.

I nodded, breathing heavily.

We hurried to the bikes. This time I did take her hand. Soon we were mounted and she took the lead. Five minutes later we were spinning into the parking lot of a small apartment complex. I saw her little red Wrangler. She opened the door and pushed her bike inside. I left mine out on the sidewalk and followed her in. She'd leaned her bike against the living room wall and as our eyes met I could see that she was having second thoughts. She stood facing me.

"Penny," I said. "If you don't want to do this it's okay."

She shook her head and turned to walk down the hallway, signing me to follow her. "Give me a few minutes," she said. She entered the bathroom, gesturing to an open doorway to her right. When I got there I saw that it was her bedroom. She closed the bathroom door.

I stood in the doorway of her bedroom for a minute or two, attempting to make sense of all the emotions tearing around inside me. And then I took off my clothes. I lay down on the bed and then got up again to extract the two condoms from my wallet. I lay down, listening for sounds of movement. Nothing. The minutes passed. Maybe she escaped through a back window, I thought. After waiting some more I got up and knocked on the bathroom door.

"Yes?" She said.

"I wanted to make sure you were still alive," I said. "By the way, they're this amazing shade of indigo right now."

I heard jerky spurts of urine hitting water and muffled laughter. "Jesus, Stephen."

I lay down once more and a couple of minutes later she came out. She was naked. I was enthralled by the sight of her full body moving towards me. She'd let down her hair and it hung, thick and straight, past her shoulders.

"You're a nut," she said. She sat down on the edge of the bed and put her hand on my stomach, rubbing lightly. I reached out to touch her thigh. Her hand slid down and took hold of my growing hardness, gently stroking. Then she leaned over and took me in her mouth. The enveloping sensation of moist warmth made me groan. I ran the fingers of both hands through her silky black hair without trying to guide her. I could tell that this was something she enjoyed doing; it's obvious when a woman doesn't.

"That feels wonderful Penny." My hips kept lifting, thrusting.

"Mmmm," she said. Her right hand was moving between her

legs.

Several minutes later she pulled back and scrambled onto the bed, straddling me. I tore the condom package and rolled the latex sheath over my cock. When I was covered she reached down and held me as she sat. I slid in easily; clearly she'd been ready. She gave a deep sigh, smiling down at me before closing her eyes and leaning her head back. She moved with a sensual unselfconscious grace, seeking the places inside herself that liked to be rubbed. The part of me that was doing the rubbing wasn't complaining; I wanted the feeling her slick warmth sliding around me to last forever. Her blackberry nipples stood erect and I reached up with both hands to catch them with my fingers.

"Oh yeah," she said, talking to the ceiling. "I like them pulled. Especially when I'm coming. I like them pulled hard then."

I tugged them, giving her breasts an odd pointed shape. She groaned. "Lean down, honey," I said. "I want to taste them."

I could feel the soft heat of her belly against mine. I took one of the thick berries in my mouth. She sighed as I sucked. I let go and blew lightly across the wet surface.

"Ooooh," she said. "That's a new one." And offered me the other nipple. I gave it the same treatment. My neck was feeling a little strained so I fell back against the pillow. Her mouth found mine and her small hot tongue probed between my lips. I sucked it in, tasting her sweetness. My hands clutched her back, exploring her smooth skin from shoulders to bottom. I grasped a full cheek in each hand and squeezed. I could feel her respond. My tongue was in her mouth now and she sucked it fervently.

"I'm going to make myself come now," she said, pushing herself up.

"Oh, yeah, ride me Baby."

With a look of intense concentration, eyes closed, she began to rock back and forth on top of me. I grabbed her nipples with my fingers.

"Yes. Yes," she moaned. "Pull them hard. Pinch them." I was happy to comply.

She was moving faster. Grunting. Beads of sweat had popped out on her upper lip. I was thrusting to meet her as best I could while yanking at her thick nipples.

"Oh shit. I'm so close," she said. "Oh shit."

I reached down and fumbled to find her clitoris.

"Oh, I'm coming. Oh yes." Her body went through the same movements I'd seen when she masturbated. Clenching and quivering. Then she settled over me like a slow heavy rain. I could feel random quavers jump through her muscles for a couple of minutes. And then she was still.

"You didn't come, did you?" She said into my ear.

"No, honey."

"I assume you want to."

"Yes, honey."

"You are a nut. Any special way you'd like to do it?"

"I've found that doggy style works best for me. For some reason."

"Okay. I like that one."

We lay quietly for several more minutes. My hands explored her soft skin. Her fingers played in my hair. And then she rolled over on her back beside me. Something about the way she looked gave me a sudden urge. I sat up and moved until I was kneeling between her legs, gently pushing them open. She understood my intentions.

"Mmmm. I was hoping you'd do that," she said. Spreading herself.

I lay down on my stomach, cupping her bottom in my hands, and looked at her. The black hairs were short and sparse. The puffy outer lips had divided to reveal that the inner labia were dark, like her nipples. The opening below was a rich glistening pink. I leaned in to taste her. She was delicious. "Yum," I said.

"I'm glad you like it," she said. "Really glad." Laughter in her voice.

I teased the delicate inner lips with my tongue with occasional circling journeys around her hard little clitoris. She sighed over and over, her hips lifting involuntarily. Her fingers were tangled in my hair clutching my head. I pressed my tongue into her depths.

"Oh yes," she moaned. Clutching me tighter. I thought I felt her come. A small one.

I continued for awhile longer. Loving the taste of her. She had what I took to be another small orgasm.

Then, on my hands and knees, I moved up her body, kissing as I went until I reached her mouth. Our lips met and I could feel her eagerness and gratitude. We played the tongue sucking game again. When I lifted my head to breath she turned over, pushing past my leg and arm, and positioned herself so that her butt was in the air. Presenting.

"Nearer the edge of the bed," I said. "So I can stand on the floor."

Catching my drift she backed up until her feet and ankles

extended over the side. I got off the bed, adjusting the condom over a revitalized erection, and moved up behind her. I was stimulated by the view of her wide rounded bottom framing the cleft of her pussy. I reveled in feeling the smooth softness of her skin. Her hand came out from between her legs and grasped me, pulling me towards her opening. I laughed for a second. But feeling her creamy heat closing around me withered my amusement. This was serious business.

"Oh God, Penny," I sighed. I began thrusting. I grasped her hips to make the in-going strokes harder, deeper. She pushed to meet me. Our bodies smacked together.

"Yes. Yes. Yes." She was groaning into the bedspread each time I buried myself fully.

I was only thinking about my own pleasure right now. She'd had her fun. My world had been reduced to the exquisite friction of feeling a nerve-rich part of my body moving inside the welcoming, and happily juicy, part of hers. And the sight of her brown back, and broad behind, and her black hair spilling across the counterpane. I looked down to watch our connection. Seeing how the opening of her vagina gripped me each time I withdrew. It was all I needed.

"I'm coming, Penny."

"Mmmm. Yes."

And I was. I was transfixed by the profound pulsing jets of my release. I groaned and held her tight against me. And then the pleasure faded. I slumped against her bottom and she collapsed beneath me. After a minute or so I shifted until I was lying next to her with my leg across her bottom and my arm on her back. I dozed for a time and awoke to feel her moving out from under me. Standing beside the bed she turned on the light.

"Stephen, it's almost dark. I'll drive you home," she said. She padded across the room and into the bathroom. The image of her flowing black hair and brown body, viewed from behind, stuck with me. I slowly got off the bed and put on my clothes. Again she was in the bathroom for a long time. I wondered what she did in there. The doorbell rang. "Could you get that Stephen," she called. "I'll be right out."

I opened the door. A tall man with curly brown hair stared at me with surprise.

"Is Angel here?" He said after hesitating.

"This is Penny's apartment," I said, assuming he had the wrong place. Penny came up beside me.

"You must mean," she said, stopping. "She moved. Out of state."

I had no idea who she was talking about.

He looked at us. It was clear that this news was a shock to him. "Did she leave a forwarding address?"

"No," Penny said. "I'm sorry."

He looked at us a moment longer and then turned to go. Penny closed the door.

"Have you got everything?" She asked me. "As soon as he leaves I'll take you home." A minute later we heard his car start up and pull away. She opened the door and we attached my bike to the rack that was mounted on her vehicle. She drove me to my place. Neither of us said much. Once we'd taken my bike off the car I gave her a hug and we kissed. But she seemed distant. I felt a sense of foreboding as I watched her drive away.

PENNY ARRIVED at work shortly after I did the next day. I'd been feeling uneasy about seeing her, unsure of how things stood between us. But she greeted me warmly although I sensed a certain reserve.

"I brought you something," she said. Some of the old sparkle in her eyes. "I'll give it to you at break time."

If her intention was to make me start to itch with curiosity she succeeded. I couldn't imagine what she'd want to give me or why. It made me realize how insecure I was feeling. At break time she beckoned me over to the side door and we walked out into the alley. She handed me a small but heavy box, like those from jewelry stores, wrapped up in ribbon. I looked at her in surprise.

"Go ahead, open it," she said, with a trace of nervousness.

When I did I found two dark blue spheres about an inch in diameter nestled in the pure whiteness of the cotton padding.

"Now you do, in fact, have blue balls," she said.

"Just what I need."

"I was visiting my friend Janey last Monday. She teaches ceramics at the community college. And one of her students made these for some project or other and then left them. When I saw them I thought of you."

"I'm flattered. I think," I said. We laughed but something had happened to the ease we used to feel with each other.

"The glaze is called Cobalt Blue," she said. "Janey said they were high fired. Whatever that means." We stood for a moment, both of us looking down at the two blue globes.

"You want to hang out after work?" I said. I felt her withdraw.

"I'm sorry Stephen," she said. "I've got a bunch of stuff to do this afternoon."

As we walked back into the restaurant I knew that the magic bubble of delight that had enclosed us had burst. For reasons I couldn't begin to grasp. It made me feel desperate, and sad. We passed through the door and it was as if I'd entered a thick haze. The day went by in a blur.

I asked her again the next morning. And got the same answer. The next day, Sunday, she called in sick.

"I'M LEAVING," she said. "Going back to Arizona. I gave my notice two weeks ago. This is my last day."

I felt as if I'd been kicked in the stomach. Hard. Again we were standing in the alley. It was break time on Monday.

"I'm sorry Stephen," she said. "I've dreaded telling you. I kept putting it off."

I looked away to hide the tears but she seemed to know that they were there.

"I guess I made it worse. God, I'm sorry. I never expected this to happen. I shouldn't have let things go so far."

"I don't find it easy to make friends," I said, trying to cover up the roughness in my voice. "And I've enjoyed being with you so much."

"I know. I've enjoyed being with you too. That's why we're in this mess," she said with a short sorrowful laugh. "I don't usually get carried away like this. I think maybe it was because I knew I was leaving. It made me feel free somehow."

"What? Free to leave me high and dry?"

"I can't be the only woman in town who'd like to be your friend." Her voice was full of anger now. "You know, if you'd simply talk to people. Being friendly is not that hard. I'm sure you can find someone."

I walked away. I didn't want to hear.

We avoided each other, as best we could, for the rest of the day. She left before I did. I watched her ride her bike through the courtyard toward the street and wondered if I'd ever see her again.

Several times, in the next few days, without planning to, I found myself halfway to her apartment. Each time I turned around. Nothing I thought of to say to her would have made any difference.

Now, as I recollected all the things we'd done, I realized that her abrupt shifts in mood made sense. They'd been moments when she became aware that I had expectations that she would not be able to fulfill. It helped me to know that this had been troubling to her.

I could have stayed angry. I could have been very angry if I'd given it half a chance. She'd known all along that she was leaving and hadn't told me. She'd told Vicente. But not me. I was hurt, that was undeniable. But I chose not to be angry. Although, more than once, I became conscious of being on the edge of a storm of rage.

What truly mattered? That was the question that kept coming up for me. Did I want to rant and rave about something I perceived as a betrayal or did I want to treasure the moments we'd had. It was obvious to me that I couldn't do both. I had to choose one or the other.

I did feel hurt. I did feel abandoned. I was deeply disappointed that my dreams of our becoming close friends would never happen. But I chose to treasure the memories. The heart warming memories. I knew the healing wouldn't happen all at once, that I'd continue to grieve.

I set you free little bird, I thought to myself, late Thursday night. Not without a deep stab of pain. Not without some residual anger.

THE DOORBELL RANG late Friday afternoon. Harold and Maude ran to investigate; Harold climbed behind the blinds in the front window to get a good view. When I opened the door Penny was standing halfway down the sidewalk with her hands in the back pockets of her jeans and her arms akimbo. Despite the open stance there was a look of wariness in her face, as if she was afraid of what I'd do.

"I came to say goodbye," she said.

I glanced up to see her Jeep Wrangler, with a U-Haul trailer attached, parked in the street. The engine running. I stepped through the doorway, making sure the cats stayed inside, and closed the door. For a minute we stood facing each other. I was intimidated by her reserve. And then my heart was flooded with the realization that this would probably be the last time I'd ever see her again. Taking a couple of steps I put my arms around her shoulders and pulled her against me. "I'm going to miss you Penny."

She was rigid for a couple of seconds and then her hands came out of her pockets and slid around me. She hugged me tight, burying her face against my shoulder. "Yeah, I'll miss you too," came her muffled voice.

I savored the feeling of her sturdy body pressing along the length of mine. I stroked her back. Until, finally, she pulled away.

"You have my address," I said. "I'd love to hear from you. Know how you're doing."

"I'll try to write."

Her dark eyes were opaque. I sensed that it was unlikely to happen. She lifted her arm and we shook hands. It was an awkward gesture. And then she turned, walked around the front of the Jeep, and climbed in without another glance. The little caravan halted at the stop sign at the end of the street, the taillights flashing in the twilight. Then she was turning. Then she was gone.

I stood gazing across the railroad tracks until I saw the Jeep and trailer on the street beyond, heading for the Interstate. Within seconds it disappeared. "Goodbye Penny," I said.

I remained standing at the edge of the sidewalk, letting darkness settle around me. "Thank you," I whispered. I sighed. I turned to go in. She'd left me with sweet memories. Such sweet memories. And balls of cobalt blue.

I Never Promised You A Zipless Fuck

Part 1:

"What I've learned is that when a man mentions sex in a personal ad he wants to get laid," Angel said with a slight smile.

He looked at her, more than a little taken aback. He thought that this had been dealt with. "Okay, I mentioned sex. But it was only to say I wasn't interested in one night stands," he said. "As I told you in my emails I'm looking for friends. I would like sex, or at least being able to openly talk about sex, to be a part of the friendship. But, Angel, what I want more than anything is to find people I enjoy hanging out with. I thought you understood that."

"Yes, well," she said, "most guys I know talk all kinds of shit but only want one thing."

He looked at her again. This was not going well, as far as he was concerned. Physically he found her very attractive but they seemed to be at cross purposes.

"I don't know about other guys," he said, finally. "All I do know I want more than some kind of zipless fuck. I need an emotional connection. I thought women liked that."

"You're weird," she said. But for the first time there was genuine amusement in her voice.

Two weeks ago she'd responded to an ad he had on an Internet dating site. They'd exchanged a number of emails and come to the mutual conclusion that they'd like to meet. So here they were, having met for the first time at the restaurant she'd suggested.

"Well, yes, I know I'm kind of a complicated guy," he said in response to her comment. "As I told you in my emails I'm not a one woman man. But I don't play games. You'll always know where you stand with me." She grinned at him. The realization that she might be jerking his chain slowly dawned. "You're weird," she said again. "But very interesting. And you seem nice, for a weird person." She paused. "So, what kinds of things do you like to do with your friends?"

"Oh, I don't know," he said, "hang out, go for walks, watch videos, talk."

"Have sex?" She said, looking into his eyes. He felt his pulse quicken and his cock begin snaking down his pants leg.

"If that's something we both want to do." He felt something touch his ankle and guessed it was one of her feet. He tried to discreetly adjust his cock, now almost hard, but had the impression that she knew exactly what was going on. Whatever was under the table had found his knee.

"How many friends are we talking about here?" She asked, looking mischievous. He liked the warm sparkle in her eyes, the sense of vitality and intelligence.

"I'm kind of in the middle of a dry spell right now," he said, feeling foolish. "The women I've met so far weren't too thrilled with the idea of polyamory."

"Polyamory?"

"I'm sure I mentioned it," he said. "Whoever coined the word mixed the Greek 'poly' and the Latin 'amor'; it means, basically, 'many loves'. Swinging is, in essence, about sex. Polyamory includes a deeper emotional involvement."

"Oh yeah, I remember now," she said. The presence pulled away from his knee and a moment later the waitress was placing their food in front of them.

"So," she said after the waitress had left and they began to eat. "When was the last time you got any?" He almost choked. The presence was back, edging up the inside of his thigh.

He looked at her, wanting to lie but being the sort of person he was he knew he wouldn't.

"Alan?" She said with mock severity.

"Over a year," he muttered.

The thing under the table disappeared. Her eyes were round with surprise. "You talk about all these 'friends' and I thought···"

"Well, I have some friends online and we do things. You know, chat and webcams, but it's all long distance. I haven't been with anyone physically for over a year." He hated hearing the defensiveness in his voice. "Finding like-minded women in this area is difficult. At least it is for me."

"You poor baby," she said quietly with a hint of humor. "I think it's time you dropped your fork."

"What?"

"Drop your fork."

He didn't drop his fork but got the drift of her suggestion. With a furtive glance around to see if anyone was watching he leaned over and looked under the table. Her knee-length dress was pulled up to the middle of her thighs and her legs were open. It took him a moment to realize what he was looking at. She was bare. Not only was there no underwear. There was no hair. Blood rushed to two places, his cock and his face. She laughed when she saw his red face rising over the edge of the table.

"You like?" She asked.

Speechless, he nodded. He wanted to tell her how much he enjoyed her playful spirit but couldn't quite get his tongue to cooperate.

"I'm so wet right now," she said in a low husky voice. "Would you like to go to my place?"

His heart was hammering. He nodded again. This was his kind of friend.

They left their almost untouched plates behind. He paid and they hurried out of the restaurant.

"We can walk to my apartment from here," she said, taking his hand. They walked the block and a half, in an intense silence. At the door she fumbled with her keys, trying two before she got the right one. Once inside the door they embraced. He slid his hands up under her dress, feeling the smooth softness of her naked bottom. They kissed. She was moaning. He could feel her reaching around behind him and the room was filled with light. She broke off the kiss and dragged him down the hall. In the next instant the bedroom light was on and he could see a large bed, neatly made up, and a blur of pastel colors. Angel was pulling her dress over her head, kicking off her shoes. Naked she leapt onto the bed.

It took him a moment longer. He was overdressed with a t-shirt, jeans, underwear, socks, and shoes. She watched as his body was revealed with frank interest while massaging her full breasts. And then they were delighting in the feel of bare skin pressed against bare skin.

"Oh God." He said. "I've missed this so much." He was pulling her tight against him, rubbing his hands over her back and buttocks. They kissed, mouths open. Sucking each other's tongue in turn. He felt her hand close around his cock. His fingers discovered her creamy smoothness. With a groaning sigh she extricated herself and, belly down on the bed, reached over the edge to paw through her purse on the floor. He rose up on his knees and stared down at her, drinking in the sight of her very female body. Her broad behind. Then once more his fingers were buried in her hot creamy smoothness.

"Ahhh. Ahhh." She sighed, pushing against his hand. One of her arms was reaching up and he saw that she was holding a condom. He took it from her, tore the package with his teeth, and began putting it on his cock. And then she was there, helping him. The moment it was on she was falling back, legs open, arms welcoming. He slid inside her.

They moaned simultaneously as they felt their bodies join.

He wrapped his arms around her and they moved together. He almost felt like crying because of the intensity of the feeling. He didn't last long but he didn't have to. She was there with him. They fell into a damp heap. Next he was lying on his back with her head on his shoulder and her body close against his. And then he was asleep.

He woke up in the darkness. She was somewhere above him. He was hard and her hand was around his cock. She lowered herself onto him but something was different. She was moving up and down and squeezing his cock with an unusual tightness. "Oh yeah, oh yeah, oh yeah," she grunted each time she came down. He reached out to touch her and was shocked by a sudden understanding. She'd put him in her ass. It was clearly something that she enjoyed very much. He, however, although the physical pleasure was undeniable, had mixed feelings about anal sex. An inner part of himself withdrew.

She moved faster and faster. The thought entered his head that she must be an athlete of some sort because of how well she controlled her body. Her hands grasped the sides of his rib cage; she pounded herself down onto him. He could tell that she was getting close because of the sounds she was making. Harsh grunts. Growls. Then she was keening with the pleasure of release. Hearing her made him come too. And he fell asleep again.

The next time he awoke she was shaking him. "I'm sorry but you need to leave. My roommate will be home soon and it would be easier if you weren't here. I'm sorry."

"That's okay, I understand," he said sleepily. After he'd climbed back into his clothes and they'd walked to the door he hugged her. She was still naked. "I'm looking forward to our being friends," he said. They kissed.

"You're a sweet guy," she responded. Later, when he

remembered her saying this, he heard a note of regret. He stepped out into the night and began walking back to the restaurant where he'd left his car.

He sent her an email the next morning, thanking her for the delightful evening. She didn't reply. He sent another a week later. Still nothing. He felt a sharp pang of disappointment each time he thought of her. It had meant so much to him to believe that he'd found a friend. In the two weeks that they'd been in contact he'd grown to like her more and more. And he'd thought she liked him too.

About three weeks after their meeting he went to the apartment she'd taken him to and knocked. A young man dressed in black opened the door.

"Is Angel here?"

"Angel?" The young man looked confused. "This is Penny's place." A Native American woman with a broad face and lively brown eyes came up behind him. "He's looking for someone named Angel," he told her.

"You must mean, uh, she moved out of town," the young woman said with a guarded expression.

"Did she leave a forwarding address?" Alan asked.

"No, I'm sorry, she didn't." They watched him absorb this news.

"Well, thanks. Sorry to bother you," he said. The door closed.

Over time the sting receded. He thought of her now and again. It was a special memory; there weren't a lot of people who caught his attention as quickly and deeply as she had. He'd liked her. A lot.

As time passed things changed. He made some new friends. He started having a regular sex life again.

Part 2:

Then she sent him an email:

Hello Alan, I don't know if you'll remember me. We met very briefly over two years ago. I left Silver City a short time after we were together and I've regretted the way I treated you. I didn't even say goodbye. I'd like to apologize, if you'll let me. Angie

He sent this response:

Hi Angie, If you're the woman I knew as Angel I do remember you. Fondly. If you are, in fact, the same woman I will happily accept your apology. Alan

She replied:

Hi Alan, I'd forgotten I'd introduced myself as Angel. How

strange. Yes, we're the same woman. I'm very sorry for the way things ended between us. I know you were looking for something ongoing. You said so more than once. And I led you on. I hate to say it but it's true. I knew I was leaving at the time but I went right ahead even though I knew that you didn't want a one night stand. All I can say in my defense is that I was going through some stuff back then and I was more than a little pissed at men. And I took it out on you. I shouldn't have. I'm sorry. I really really am. The funny thing, Alan, is that I've never been able to get you out of my system. You fucker! (LOL with tears of regret in my eyes) You're a neat guy. Strange but neat. And I've been reading up on that polyamory business you told me about and I'm liking it more and more. I don't know if you can forgive me. And I don't know what I expect to happen even if you can. But I needed to apologize if only to feel better about myself.   Angie

In return he wrote:

Hi Angie, Yes, I can forgive you. I know that people have reasons for doing what they do even though those reasons aren't always clear to the people their decisions affect. But, ultimately, you aren't responsible for my happiness. I am. So, despite my disappointment, I can accept what you did. And the truth is that I liked you a lot. That never stopped. I hope this makes sense. But one other thing that needs to be addressed. The thing that disturbed me most about our encounter was when you put my cock in your ass without asking me if you could. I felt used. It seemed to me that you didn't care about how I might feel about it. This might not bother other men but it bothers me. Alan

Her response came within hours:

Oh Alan, Jeez, I'd forgotten about that too. Yes, I can see why you felt the way you did. To the best of my recollection I didn't mean anything by it. I guess it was another part of using you. Which I believe I've admitted I did. And of course I apologize. Again. You have to understand that I started feeling bad about the way I treated you almost at once. I remember your saying something about our being friends when you left and, because I knew I was leaving town, I felt about two inches tall. They say that absence makes the heart grow fonder and in your case it's true. The more I've thought about you the more I've regretted what I did. And the more I've liked you. I think I've learned my lesson. It won't happen again. Angie

He replied:

Hi Angie, Apology accepted. I'm glad we're friends again. Where are you living now? Your friend, Alan

And she sent this in return:

Alan, my friend, I'm living in Terra Haute, Indiana. Pretty far away. Kisses, Angie

He zinged back:

Hello sweet Angie, Indiana!!!!! What the *@$& are you doing there? I wasn't expecting for there to be quite so much distance between us. Kisses and hugs, Alan

For the next three months they corresponded regularly. Often exchanging emails two or three times a day. He told her about his job and about Esther and Johanna, his new friends. She seemed interested so he shared more details. She didn't balk. When he and the two women experimented with a threesome he relayed a short account of their activities, with Johanna and Esther's permission, to Angie. She said it sounded like fun and to tell her more.

In return she revealed the day to day happenings of her life in Indiana. She told him about her work and her social life. Twice she mentioned casual sexual encounters she'd had, taking pains to assure him that she'd made it clear to her partners what they could expect of her. He asked if she'd enjoyed herself. She said she had.

Sometime towards the end of the second month of their correspondence, realizing he had a weeks vacation time coming, he broached the possibility of a visit. Her first response was total delight. A little later she began expressing some trepidation and said she was worried about letting him down again. He told her that he was quite willing to take his chances.

During the third month they began playing with cybersex and phonesex. It was obvious that the old spark was still there. Hearing the sounds over the phone of the other in the throes of orgasm made the distance hard to bear.

She was standing beyond the metal detectors as he strode down the airport hallway after disembarking. He recognized her at once. And saw her eyes light up when she saw him. There was a moment of awkwardness. They stood facing each other. And then they were wrapped in a tight embrace.   "You feel so good," he said.

"Ummm, so do you."

"Are you wearing panties?" He whispered in her ear.

She burst into laughter. "As a matter of fact I am. A thong, anyway."

"Not for long," he said.

"I'm looking forward to being thongless," she said in a low voice charged with sexual meaning. That was all it took to make him hard.

After picking up his luggage she drove him to her apartment. The scene that followed was very similar to their first time. Because she'd gained some weight she was shyer about her body and, due to the hurt he'd experienced before, he was more tentative but these things created only temporary setbacks. Soon they were once more moving together, sharing the sweet pleasure their bodies made. She asked if he would take her anally and he was happy to give her that gift.

The week passed all too quickly. They spent as much time talking as they did having sex. So, though neither of them felt the issues between them had been entirely resolved, it became clear that the bond that had survived two years of estrangement was real. They agreed that they were well on the way to becoming true friends.

"I can't make any promises but I'm thinking of moving back to Silver City," she said at the end of his visit. They were standing in the airport.

"If you do you've got a friend," he said. "I can't promise any more than that. And sex, if you want it."

"Oh, I'll want it," she said, with a husky edge to her voice that made his balls tingle. Their eyes locked and they both smiled.

"You'll have to share me with Johanna and Esther, you know," he said.

"Oh Jesus," she said, "For something that seemed pretty simple at the time this has gotten awfully complicated."

"Well hey." He said, before turning to board the plane, "I never promised you a zipless fuck."

He loved to hear her laugh.

A Huge One Could Be Yours

"A Huge One Could Be Yours," the email read. "A bigger penis in 60 days or your money back."

Yeah, right, I thought. Do they actually get enough poor schmucks buying their line to make any money? But I didn't hit the delete key. Something kept me sitting there. The other day I'd walked into our bedroom to find my wife Katie looking through her collection of John Holmes magazines and playing with herself. It made me feel a bit inadequate; I know I'm not the only guy that the late great J.H. has made insecure.

"Shit, it's only $19.95. Even if it doesn't work it's not going to break me," I decided. So I pulled out my credit card and ordered.

Later that evening I told Katie what I'd done. "Oh, Hon," she said, "I like your cock the way it is. Sure I like to fantasize sometimes about having a really big one inside me but I love you Jon for who you are."

Oh, right, I thought. I smiled at her, my male ego bruised black and blue. A really big one. Just you wait.

Four days later a priority mail package arrived. I opened it with mixed feelings; on one hand I felt like a complete fool for letting myself fall for such age old scam while on the other there was the persistent gleam of hope that soon I'd be able to satisfy my wife in a way she'd never been satisfied before. That soon she would worship unquestioningly at the protruding alter of my manhood.

The instructions were absurd. The basis of the treatment was a tube of cream that was supposed to be applied on the penis once a day. The kit also contained several pairs of rubber gloves and a dire warning, printed in large red letters, that said that the cream must not make contact with any other part of the body before the ten minute drying period was up or that part too would become permanently enlarged. "In your dreams," I scoffed. But I followed the instructions carefully.

A couple of days later, after no signs of enlargement had made themselves visible I reread the info sheet and found, hidden away on the back, the small print where it said, "May not work for everyone." "Should be 'may not work for anyone' " was my bitter comment. And yet I continued to apply the cream until it was gone, better to be a total fool than a dummy who gives up too easily.

Two more weeks passed. Katie and I were making the beast with two backs when she said, "Jon, it feels bigger." I pulled out of her, turned on the light, and looked. She looked too. It was bigger. "Oh shit," she said, putting her hand around it. "How big is it going to get?"

"I don't know," I said. But I resolved to go online the next morning and order five more tubes of cream.

Once they came I began doing the treatments three times a day until I'd used up all five tubes. Katie couldn't get enough of me. She'd pull me aside at odd moments eager to open my pants and make me hard. Strangely enough my cock when flaccid was no bigger than it ever had been but when it became erect it was substantially larger, to say the least. Katie loved looking at how big and thick it was, holding it in her hands, and taking the head in her mouth. If I was too fatigued to fuck at night she'd tease and suck my cock until it rose to its full glory and then she'd ride me from orgasm to orgasm moaning about how full it made her feel. Eat your late great heart out, John Holmes, I thought. Little did I know that I'd soon be sinking my teeth into my own.

The night came, almost eight weeks after I'd begun using the cream, when my cock wouldn't fit inside her. It was a terrible night. She grunted and strained for hours to take me inside but it wouldn't work. She was raging with frustration, drops of sweat from her forehead dropping onto my chest. I lay on my back with a cold clammy hand of fear making a tight fist around my heart. I knew then I'd made a horrible mistake. Now all I could do was ride the tiger of my folly to learn my final fate.

Our marriage fell apart two months after that disastrous night. And my cock continued to grow. I walked in mortal fear of becoming aroused. More times than I care to think about I had to run to the men's room or some other private place to let myself out before this demon I'd nurtured ripped my pants apart.

At work my vivacious young secretary, Heather Crawford, hearing through the grapevine that my wife had left me, conceived the idea that the quickest and easiest route to inordinate conspicuous consumption was to become my trophy wife. To that end she began to flaunt her considerable charms. She made my life a living hell. I spent more time in the men's room than at my desk. I'm sure she found this puzzling but I was not in a state of mind to confront anything with confidence and dispatch.

I will always remember with burning shame the day she turned in her chair with studied negligence and revealed to me that she wasn't wearing underwear. I can still hear, as if it were only a moment ago, the loud ripping sound of my trousers being torn away as my cock engorged at the sight of those delicate lips, bare shaven, parted to reveal the glimmer of pink.

I stood there clutching at the flying shreds of my clothing. Heather screamed frantically, standing up and backing away from me until a wall blocked her escape. It was clear that the prospect of being my trophy wife had instantaneously lost its savor. The room filled with people, all of them staring goggle-eyed at my monstrous member. If I'd have had a gun then I would have shot myself.

An hour or so later, after I'd swathed myself in the red velvet curtain from the conference room, I was asked to clear out my desk and never come back. Roderick Laidlaw III, the VP in charge of personnel, told me that the phrase "sexual harassment" didn't begin to describe the extent of my transgression. "This is more like all out war," he said. "The expression from the last conflict with Iraq 'shock and awe' might be most appropriate."

I won't go into all the hurtful and humiliating details of my personal decline in the period during which my cock reached the zenith of its expansion. I did manage to find a way to support myself using the Internet to work out of my small shabby apartment. And I took to wearing muu muus in public, the very few times I went out among my fellow human beings, because they tented instead of tearing which, while still embarrassing, wasn't as traumatic as being totally exposed.

As I neared the bottom of my sad trajectory I had one short period of hope. I stumbled across a site called Grownup Fun Finder in which I spotted a number of profiles submitted by women seeking men with large cocks. My heart leaped up. I sent out initial contact emails and wrote my own profile to put on the site with burning enthusiasm. And I got many many emails in return as well as those from women responding to my profile. They all asked for a photo to substantiate my claims. Oh happy day. But apparently they thought that I, like other men they'd encountered, had grossly misrepresented my attributes. "Grotesque!" "I like 'em big but not THAT big." "Never contact me ever again!" Was the upshot of those few replies I got. I never heard from most of them after the pic was sent. I'd now sunk to the lowest point.

I'd inserted a round in the chamber of the gun I'd bought at a local gun show. I was lifting it to my head when⋯ I got an email.

It was a woman responding to my profile on Grownup Fun Finder. She said she was only a moment away from swallowing twenty sleeping pills and washing them down with a quart of vodka. I was her very last hope, she said. Her husband, she informed me, had used the same cream I had and had kept wanting to fuck her five minutes after he'd put on the cream. Handling his cock made him randy, she explained. Now her cunt was a yawning chasm but his cock hadn't changed at all. He was one of the people on which the cream didn't work although, like me, he'd bought tube after tube of the stuff.

Through a fog of suicidal ennui I desultorily emailed her a copy of my photo and went back to gazing into the black hole at the end of my revolver. Half an hour. I'll give her half an hour, I thought to myself.

Only seven minutes later my computer told me I had mail. "Omigod!" the email read. "Don't shoot yourself, please. My prayers have been answered. Do you have instant messaging? Do you have a webcam?" I had both. We exchanged handles and linked up. I was beginning to feel a little excited. I put my pistol on the floor beside my chair. Then I saw her. She was fucking herself with three metal baseball bats bound together with duct tape. My cock rose, lifting up my desk and dumping my monitor on the floor. I leaned over the upturned desk to see that she'd seen my prodigious dong and had redoubled her efforts. I was stroking myself as best I could with both hands, one on each side of my cock. I was screaming and I could see her mouth too was wide open. It felt so satisfying to know that there was a place in the world where I'd find a perfect fit. A thick white stream shot out of me and slapped against the wall four feet away. It felt so good to finally be able to let go, knowing I wasn't alone. Two more spurts shot out.

"Where do you live?" I messaged her as soon as I stopped shaking long enough to type.

"Nevada," she replied, adding her complete address.

I grabbed my Rand McNally and made some quick calculations. "I'll be there in about 10 hours," I messaged.

"I'll be waiting Baby; bring that big boy to me," she responded.

I drove like a maniac leaving almost every trace of my old life behind me. Every time I thought of her, and of that sweet pink cavernous tunnel, I'd have to lean to the side to be able to see around the fabric draped pillar in front of me. I made the trip in eight hours and forty two minutes. I screeched to a stop in her driveway and saw that her door was wide open. I jumped out of the car and rushed inside, pulling up my muu muu as I ran. There she lay, naked, legs akimbo. I buried myself in her with a keening wail. It was like being a virgin again.

We got married the next day. Nevada is the state that makes these things easy. We figure we'll make it work one way or another. We don't have much choice. After two years neither of our genitalia show any signs of shrinkage.

Cabin In the Woods

In talking with her friend Debbie, Linda mentioned her desire to get away from things for awhile. Almost the moment the words left her lips Debbie's face lit up.

"I've got a little cabin outside of El Dorado Springs that I'd be happy to let you use for as long as you need. I might even join you for a day or two," her friend said. After a short conversation the decision was made.

It took almost the whole month of May to work out all the mundane details of getting vacation time, making sure her son was taken care of, and gathering together the items she wanted to take with her. Not the least of these being her vibrator and 8" dildo. All that was done now and she was anticipating a week and a half of solitary freedom. Although she did felt a small pang of regret that she couldn't share it with a true kindred spirit.

She'd arrived late in the afternoon of the day before yesterday and found her friend's cabin to be rustic and comfortable. Electricity was supplied by a small but adequate solar system, and there was a composting toilet. In the living room was a stereo and a good collection of CDs. All that was lacking, which was fine with her, was a television and a telephone.

Since her arrival she'd been basking in the knowledge that there was nothing she had to do except loaf and invite her soul. There'd been something lusciously wicked yesterday about lying naked in bed at almost noon with the windows open to the sunshine and the redolence of pine. She'd brought herself to one powerful orgasm. And then another.

Today she felt a little more ambitious. After eating her breakfast on the small patio beside the hot tub she'd decided she was going to take a walk into the woods and explore her new surroundings. So now, dressed in a t-shirt, shorts, and sturdy shoes, she was taking the path which led through the trees. The terrain was hilly and the woods were thick but not overgrown with underbrush. Occasionally there would be a break in the trees and she'd look out over a grassy meadow, thick with flowers. She couldn't see any sign of another human being.

High above, however, a hawk was surveying a wide expanse of land in search of prey. His eyes caught sight of two people moving, unknowingly, towards each other.

It was after she'd been walking for almost an hour that she came to the small stream. She was a bit tired and wanted to find a place to rest. She walked downstream along the bank of the creek until she came to a spot where a meadow opened out on her left. To her right, on the far side of the stream, was a tall limestone cliff. Below the cliff the flow had cut a large depression in the rock that was filled with water. A natural pool. Trees nearby filtered the sunlight. She dipped her hand into the pool and found that the water was warm. She looked around, biting her lip.

She was tempted to do something she'd never done. With her heart pounding she pulled her t-shirt over her head. It made her feel exposed to be standing there in her bra. And then, with another look around, she slid off her bra. It made her feel even more exposed but also free in a way she'd never felt before. She cupped her breasts in her hands, feeling the weight of their smooth softness. Then she sat on an outcropping of rock beside the pool and took off her shoes and socks. Barefoot she stood up, hooked her shorts and panties with her thumbs, and pushed them to her feet. Stepping out of them made her feel very aware of the sensual reality of her body. She felt vividly alive. Moments later she was lying up to her neck in the water's amniotic warmth.

Around her nature flowed languidly on, drowsy in the heat. Birds called, so much a part of the ambiance that it was as if they hadn't broken the silence. She could hear the buzz and hum of insects.

Closing her eyes she softly slid her hand down between her legs. Her legs came open, almost by themselves. Her fingers began to investigate the nub of ardor, the crevices of sensation. If doing this in bed late yesterday morning had seemed wicked, doing it now opened up a sense of wildness within her that was new. She surprised herself by expressing her rich pleasure with hoarse throaty moans pulled, it seemed, from deep inside her body.

The man the hawk had seen, who was gathering sassafras to dry for his favorite tea, heard her cries. He thought he recognized the sound but found it difficult to believe that it would happen here, in the middle of the woods, far from town. Moving toward the source he found himself at the top of a steep cliff. Looking down he saw her there.

The sight of a naked woman lying in a pool with her hand between her legs stunned him. It was like a deep fantasy come to life. He was a lonely man. A man who loved women, enjoyed being around them, but whose chosen way of life was often very solitary. He felt torn. Part of him sensed that continuing to observe such a private act might make the woman feel violated. But another part, a profoundly hungry part, needed to watch her.

There was an elemental beauty about her, her breasts swaying just beneath the water's surface and the sunlight through the leaves dappling her skin, that awakened a profound wonder inside him. Her moans were clearly signaling the moment of culmination. He was barely aware that he was now erect. For a frenzied moment the water's glassy calm was broken by her agitation. The trees echoed her cries. And then there was stillness. She opened her eyes and found herself looking into his.

If anything had been the least bit different at that moment the outcome would have been changed. If she had seen him watching her as she took off her clothes she would have withdrawn into herself. If he had been less affected by seeing her, more focused on sexual titillation, his eyes would not have been so full of awe. As it was, she felt open and accepting. Proud. Wild. And he found himself responding from a corresponding place. He turned and disappeared.

She stretched blissfully, humming with the sensual fullness of her body. She knew he was coming to her. And a moment later he was there, standing among her scattered clothes, adding his to the pile. She watched with a detached interest as his slim muscled body came into view. And responded to the distinct lines of his maleness. His pants slid down and she gazed at his hard cock and swinging balls. He stepped into the water.

There was a moment of awkwardness. She began to sit up with the thought of taking him in her mouth while he gently tried to guide her to lie back against the smooth stone. Once she realized he wanted to be inside her she made him welcome. There was no need for foreplay. The first sensation of feeling him enter her, filling her, was indescribable. They both breathed in sharply and sighed as their bodies slid together. He put his arms around her and kissed her, beginning to move. The water sloshed around the edges of the pool.

He came quickly. It had been too long since he'd been with a woman. After about a minute of thrusting he groaned and stiffened. She felt him pulse inside her. And then his body went limp. She had a fleeting sense of disappointment and annoyance.

Lifting himself off her he pushed back her hair with his hand and kissed her nose. "Thank you," he said. "This is probably about the last thing I expected to happen today."

"Me too," she laughed.

"Sorry it was so quick. It'll be better next time."

She didn't reply. There was still an edge of disappointment.

He withdrew and then settled in beside her, sliding his right leg over both of hers and reached up to cover her breast with his large hand. A moment later he was kissing her. She found his soft cock and ball sack with her right hand. For long minutes they both luxuriated in the exploration of the other's body. And then she felt his cock begin to stir.

"I want to suck you," she said, giving his cock a little yank. He got the message and moved into position kneeling above her face. She could feel his cool thighs against the sides of her breasts. Water dripped from his body onto hers. His cock was showing the barest signs of hardening. She sucked the head of it into her mouth. He gave a soft moan of pleasure. She could feel his hairy ball sack rub against her chin. His cock began to swell. She looked up to meet his eyes. He smiled.

"That feels great," he said. "You like to suck cock, don't you?"

She nodded, smiling around a full mouth, loving the smooth sweet texture with the faintest hint of precum at the tip. He was almost hard now which required an adjustment. He bent over, resting his elbows on the rock above her head. She grasped the cheeks of his ass with her hands both to pull him towards her and to give herself leverage. A moment later he was hard and she slowly moved her mouth back and forth along his length, tasting him, feeling the contours of him, the ridge around the head, the bumps of the protruding veins. Her fingers played in the crack of his ass, at the entrance of the hole, and with his balls. He grunted and began to make fucking movements with his hips, sliding into her mouth. And then, suddenly, he withdrew.

"God. That was great," he said. "Now it's your turn, sweetheart." Moving back he caught her under her armpits and helped her slide up the smooth stone until her hips were out of the water. He knelt down between her legs and opened them. Wide. She bent her head and saw him staring down at her exposed womanhood. "You're beautiful," he said, looking up.

Then he was leaning down. Softly kissing the inside of her thighs. She could feel the hairs of his moustache tickling her skin. He rubbed his head of curly brown hair, threaded with grey, against her inner thighs and belly. He was taking his time. Her pussy was aching for some attention. And then the tip of his tongue gently touched her clit. And circled it. And circled it again. It was like electricity shooting out through millions of very thin wires. She grabbed his curly head with both hands and moaned, pressing his face into her throbbing cunt. She could hear him chuckling down below.

He began to make slow journeys, beginning with his tongue burrowing deep into her vagina and then rising up between her inner lips, his head shaking slightly from side to side, until his lips and tongue found her hard nub. And then he was back down in her cunt hole, rising again. He kept doing this over and over again, gradually increasing the speed. He felt her responses quickening. Then his finger was probing at her asshole. That was too much.

"Fuck me," she yelled, a bit startled by her own vehemence. "Oh God. Put it in me."

He stood up and their eyes met. She could read the fierce lust in his face and knew it was a reflection of what was in her own. And then, with one quick, almost brutal, thrust he had buried the thick shaft of his cock deep inside her cunt.

The veils had been torn away. This was primal stuff. This was Man and Woman. This was the sexual drive of the universe. Here. With him standing knee deep in water and her lying on her back on the grey stone. Here. In the sunlight that pushed through the leaves of the trees to illuminate the whiteness of their skin, their bodies melded together.

He grasped her hips with his two big hands and pushed her down against himself as his hips thrust up. She could feel the base of his belly against the lips of her cunt. He began withdrawing and thrusting. Not fast but with great power.

"Oh God yes." she cried. "Fuck me hard."

Their eyes locked. She saw the fierce lust in his and knew he was seeing the same in hers. She saw his jaw clamp tight. "You like it rough, don't you," he growled through clenched teeth. He could read her answer in her eyes.

He began fucking her. He seemed to be trying to push his whole body inside her. Hard, almost desperate, thrusts. And she opened herself wide. Wider. She wanted to swallow him. The smack of their bodies, as they hammered together in their frenzied dance, echoed against the cliff and the trees. They both were grunting

54

with the effort. Bestial raucous sounds. He grabbed the cheeks of her ass, one in each large hand, and picked her up off the stone. He pulled her down over his cock. There was a little pain but it was a stimulating pain.

This continued for long minutes. His pace kept quickening as he felt her respond. He leaned over and began tugging at her nipples with his teeth. Biting them, but not too hard. Sucking them into his mouth. Licking her breasts. Rubbing his face and hair into them, grunting.

And then, deep in her guts she could feel the thin thread of orgasm being pulled to the surface. "Oh God yes yes fuck me yes Oh God you're gonna make me cum God yes Oh yes" Her wails soared into the trees. Her cries gave him the incentive to move even faster, even more powerfully. He was snorting like a racing stallion. Thrusting hard and deep. Pounding into her. Her wailing reached a high crescendo and the waves of orgasm flowed out over her body. He gave one last pounding thrust and entered her as deep as he could go, touching her cervix. And then, following his one last hoarse gasping shout, she felt his cock throb and then his hot seed spurt into her depths. Another throb, and a weaker spurt. And a third, and final, spasm. He fell on her body as if he'd been clubbed in the head. Breathing heavily. She was too.

"Told you it would be better the next time," he managed to say into her neck. It made her laugh.

She looked up and stroked his face, brushing his long brown hair back. Kissing him softly. She became aware of the force of the sun. They were both pretty much out of the water at this point and the trees were no longer shading them. It seemed as if time had stood still, a few moments or much longer, she couldn't tell. "I think we should head up to my place," she said, feeling a sudden urge for some creature comforts. First of all something to eat. Satisfying sex made her very hungry and she was starving. And then a cool shower followed by a languid mutual massage and peaceful, long nap. All at once she realized she'd presumed that he had the time or desire to go with her, "Only if you want to, of course," she said, after a short hesitation.

"Sounds great to me," he said with a warm smile, pushing himself up and then taking her hand to pull her up also. With both of them standing he wrapped his arms around her and held her close, kissing her after making adjustments to accommodate the difference in their heights, and ran his hands over her back and bottom. She could feel his penis move against her stomach. But it didn't harden. She gave it an affectionate rub as they parted.

They each gathered their scattered clothes. Seeing that all he put back on were his socks and shoes she decided to do the same, feeling a delightful sense of freedom to be walking through the woods naked with a naked man beside her. The long walk back was punctuated with many breaks for kisses and embraces and it was late afternoon before they arrived.

After exploring the options for dinner they settled on a large salad. They shared the chores of cutting up the peppers, tomatoes, onions, cucumbers and mushrooms and tearing up the head of red leaf lettuce. He also found some feta cheese which he added and then mixed up a dressing of olive oil, wine vinegar, a touch of worcestershire sauce, garlic, pepper, and assorted herbs. And they each got a glass of iced peach tea to drink.

Neither of them felt the desire to put on clothes again, and the summer warmth made it comfortable to be naked. And since the cabin was situated more than a mile from the main road, well hidden by trees, there was no need to. They both felt a rich contentment in being able to watch the free flowing dangle and sway of the others' body. They sat down at the table on the patio and continued the conversation they'd begun over the food preparation. She told him about her son, Josh. And he told her about Amy, his daughter. They talked about their respective marriages and divorces and of the other relationships they'd had. Their eyes often met and communicated on a level all their own; they began liking each other more and more. Finishing their meal they collected the dishes and set them by the sink, too tired to deal with them that night. And after a short shared shower spent soaping each others' body, touching and tickling, and laughing like kids, they tumbled into bed and fell asleep with their bodies entwined. The massage would have to wait.

She awoke early the next morning with the sun shining into the room and a soft breeze coming through the open window. She was lying on her side facing the window. For a moment she lay absorbing the sweet smell of the air and the warmth of the sun. Then, suddenly, the events of yesterday flooded into her mind. Like images from a dream. Unreal. With profound apprehension she lifted her head and peeked over her shoulder and gave a soft sigh of relief. He was there, lying on his back with the sheet pushed away from most of his body. She turned over on her other side and looked at him, watching him sleep. She reached out and touched his chest, as if to convince herself he was there. He stirred but didn't awaken. Turning her gaze to his penis and balls the first tinglings of desire flickered inside her. Leaning over she took the head of his cock between her lips, thrilling to the first faint signs of burgeoning. With the tip of her tongue she tasted him, probing at the small hole. He moved restively. His cock was growing harder, filling her mouth. She put her hand around the shaft and held him as she sucked. She felt his hand caress her back and knew he was awake. She turned and looked up at him, still holding his cock.

"Good morning, lover," she said.

He smiled back at her, "You know how to wake a guy up right."

She went back to sucking him and he continued to caress her back. Then he reached over and indicated with his touch that he'd like her to scoot her bottom over. Without taking her mouth off him she moved herself closer and felt his hand sliding across her ass, seeking her pussy. She opened her legs to give his fingers access.

"You're wet already, sweetheart," he said.

"Hmmmm," she said.

After several more minutes of sucking him while his fingers teased her pussy lips and hard clit she moved onto her knees beside him, straddled his body, and, holding his cock straight up, looking into his eyes, slowly took his length inside herself. It felt so good. They were in a different emotional space than they were yesterday. They'd been animals in the wild yesterday. Today they were lovers. There was passion, but it was a gentle passion. A loving passion. She rose and fell on him like the movement of waves against a shore. Leaning over she gave him the gift of her breasts. A gift he gladly accepted. She could feel his hands touching her everywhere, getting to know her, holding her bottom as she moved on him. He came first and she watched his face with delight as he surrendered to his feelings of pleasure. He moaned urgently; his cock throbbed within her. He stayed hard and she continued moving until her own orgasm spilled over her with warm, sweet, gentle power. She pressed her body to his, her face in the pillow beside his neck, and he held her for several long minutes. And then she climbed off him, his cock hitting his belly with a small wet smack, and cuddled up to him with his arm around her shoulders. And they talked.

He told her that he needed to get back to his place to feed his cats and get some things done but, if it was all right with her, he would like to come back in the late afternoon or early evening. She said she'd like that. They talked of whatever came to mind, full of the glow of sexual release and their new intimacy. At last they got out of bed and he got dressed and, after giving her a long kiss and a warm hug, headed into the woods. Still naked she moved around the cabin doing some small chores feeling peaceful and restless at the same time. She liked the feeling.

When he got back that evening he found she'd put on a t-shirt, shorts, and a pair of sandals and was setting up candles around the bedroom. They enjoyed a long hug and kiss in greeting. Hand in hand they went into the kitchen; she'd already prepared some sandwiches and he put together a small salad with what was left of the vegetables and lettuce. Again they ate out on the patio and talked about what they'd done that day and about their thoughts and emotions. They learned that they both were feeling kind of shocked by the fantastical way their relationship had started and yet, they agreed, it felt comfortable. And they both hoped that it was the beginning of a long warm friendship that would include sexual intimacy. He told her, with some trepidation, that he was something of a sexual explorer and she said that that was fine with her, that she was exploring some other sexual friendships with men she'd met through the Internet.

This evening they managed to do the dishes before retiring. She lit the candles while he took a shower. And then it was her turn. She came out of the bathroom in her red robe to find him lying naked on the bed. She sat down beside him and caressed his body. He slid his hand through the labyrinth of soft cloth to find her bare skin. She leaned down to kiss him. The flames of sensual fire were fanned and the robe vanished. They moved through a variety of erotic moods from rough to gentle, from soft to fiercely passionate, learning the touches and words that caused the other to respond most powerfully. Once again they fell asleep in each others' arms.

The next morning she woke up needing to pee and made her way to the bathroom. When she was done she walked to his side of the bed and stood watching him sleep. Once again he'd kicked off the sheet and his cock and balls were in plain view. She couldn't help herself. Reaching down she touched the soft cylinder of flesh. He stirred and his eyes opened. "Good morning, sweetheart," he said, putting out his hand to touch her thigh and then moved it to her pussy. She bent to open herself to his fingers. There was the faintest hint of dampness.

After a moment she leaned over, her breasts swinging, and indicated with her hands that she wanted him to scoot over towards the middle of the bed. Once he had, she swung her leg over his head and lowered her pussy close to his face. He began to lick her, tasting slight tangy traces of urine and felt her take his soft cock in her mouth. Her fingers played with his balls. Her pillowy breasts with their protuberant nipples rubbed against the bottom of his belly. He reached down, still licking, and cupped the full smooth globes, one in each hand. The mood was one of quiet sensuality. Both of them savoring tastes and textures while at the same time enjoying the sparkles of feeling that came from the sweet activities of the other. Lazily his cock grew hard and her pussy oozed its creamy lubrication.

Taking short steps on her knees she positioned herself above his cock. He had a delightful view of her full ass and her pink open lips as she held his cock upright and then slowly eased herself down over him. Feeling her slippery heat engulfing him was enhanced by the sight of the mouth of her cunt stretching open to take him in. With a sigh she sank down till all he could see were the white cheeks of her bottom. In her depths his cock was surrounded by glowing warmth. Gripping his knees with both hands she began rocking back and forth, sighing loudly. She felt his thick length rubbing against her inner walls. He reached over her thigh and began fingering her clit. Her sighs became more pronounced. She leaned forward and he saw his shaft emerge, shiny with her juice. Then back, and his cock disappeared again.

The full focus of their attention was on the happy rubbing created by their intermingled nakedness. Each time she raised her ass her cunt seemed to close around a hungry emptiness. And then, descending, that inner void was filled with an overflowing heat. From time to time she'd sit down hard on him, savoring his probing presence in her depths and they'd quietly talk.

"God." she said, "this feels so good. I love having your cock inside me."

"Hmmm," he sighed, sliding his hands over her bottom's velvety skin, "I like being inside you."

"I could do this all day," was her breathless response.

"Sounds like a plan to me, sweetheart," he murmured. "I haven't spent a day in bed for awhile."

"I've never done that," she said, "had sex all day."

Time seemed to expand. Neither of them now felt any sense of urgency. They wrapped themselves in a warm blanket of sensuality and settled in for a long day of sweet pleasure.

That evening, spent and glowing, they sat side by side in the unheated hot tub holding hands and looking up at the night sky.

"I could get used to this," she said. "Thank you for a very special day."

"You're welcome sweetheart," he said, kissing her cheek.

"I've never cum so many times in one day in my life. Was there anything we didn't try?"

"If there is we'll have to wait to try it until tomorrow, or the day after," he said. "My cock's rubbed a little raw."

"I'm sore too, Hon. But it feels good in a funny kind of way."

"Yeah, for me too."

Sitting back in a companionable silence they each looked into the sky and followed their private thoughts. Occasionally they'd glance at each other, smile, and share gentle hand squeezes.

He stood up and stepped out of the hot tub. "I think it's about time for that massage," he said, beginning to dry himself off with one of the big towels she'd set out.

"Oh, that sounds good." She rose dripping and joined him.

While she went around the bedroom lighting candles he brought the olive oil and a small bowl from the kitchen and spread a towel on the bed. She lay face down on the towel, giggling. She wiggled her butt. He chuckled as he held the bowl of oil over a candle to warm it up. Then, putting the bowl within reach on the nightstand, he straddled her full ass, dipped his fingers into the bowl, and began to massage her shoulders. She rewarded his efforts with small grunts, moans, and sighs.

"Can you believe I'm getting hard again?"

"Mmmmm," she responded, moving her bottom.

"Feeling your soft sweet butt between my thighs is so stimulating." He continued to massage her, moving down her body until he'd done each of her feet. "Roll over," he said when he'd finished.

She rolled over and spread her legs so he could kneel between them. He massaged her front as carefully as he'd done her back. He was almost finished before he realized she'd fallen asleep. It made him smile. He looked down at her in the flickering candlelight, touched by how open and vulnerable she looked. He gazed at her pussy, seeing the faint glimmer of pink in the dim light, and thought of the day they'd shared. At times it had been passionate, like their first encounter, with raw rough sounds and words. And at other times they'd lain together barely moving, exchanging delicate caresses and gentle observations. Leaning over he kissed her clitoris. He moved out from between her legs and she muttered something, turning over on her side without waking. After extinguishing the candles he lay beside her for a long time with his hand resting on her hip before he too fell asleep.

The next morning, after a brief cuddle, they got up to take care of some of the errands that had been neglected the day before. She went into El Dorado Springs to buy groceries and he made the trek to his house to feed his cats and do some other chores. It wasn't until almost sundown that he returned and they sat down to the meal she'd prepared. They exchanged accounts of the things they'd done that day, washed the dishes, spent some time in the hot tub, and then retired to the bedroom.

They were both still rather sore but as soon as they began touching each other the passion flared to life and soon they were joined. They were in the missionary position, talking softly and looking into each others' eyes in the candlelight when something hit the floor behind them. Then a woman said, "Oh shit." Their heads swiveled at the same instant. An attractive red haired woman stood half hidden in the shadows of the doorway with her hand down her jeans.

"God Linda, I'm so sorry. I guess I got caught wet handed," the woman said, pulling her hand out of her jeans. "You guys'd never have known I was here if I hadn't hit this goddamned broom. Sorry. I'll just leave now. Shit I feel stupid." She began to turn away.

"Wait Debbie." Linda said. He realized that this must be the owner of the cabin and felt himself relax a bit.

Debbie stopped, half turned away.

Linda looked up at him. "Would you like to be with two women?"

"It wouldn't be the first time," he said. "I'm game if she is." They both turned to look at Debbie.

"Do you remember those fantasies we used to talk about? About picking up a guy?" Linda asked.

Debbie turned and looked at her for a long moment. "Yeah, I remember we used to talk about some things. Things we never did."

"Debbie, this is Ben, by the way. And Ben, as you've probably figured out, this is Debbie." Ben and Debbie glanced at each other, almost shyly, and nodded. "Well, what do you think?"

"I think my husband will shit," Debbie said with a laugh. "But what the fuck." Her hands had already begun to undo the buttons of her shirt. "Watching you guys got me hot."

Ben withdrew his cock and lay down next to Linda to observe the unveiling. Debbie gave him a humorous smirk. She pulled off her shirt, dropped it in a chair, and reached behind her back with both hands to undo her bra. He saw that she was smaller than Linda with creamy white skin and many freckles. Her breasts, when revealed, were tipped with pale pink nipples and areolas.

"You like?" Debbie said challengingly.

He turned to Linda.

"Don't look at me," Linda said, unperturbed by her friend's nakedness.

By the time he turned back to Debbie she'd kicked off her shoes and pushed her jeans and thong to the floor. She was freckled all over and her bush was a carrot colored puffball of hair.

"Yeah," he said. "I like what I see a lot."

"And I liked watching you fuck my friend Linda," Debbie said, climbing onto the bed on her knees and reaching for his cock. She was surprised to see him wince when she grabbed him.

"We're sore," Linda said. "We spent the whole day yesterday fucking. Well, off and on."

"Jeez," Debbie said. "You didn't waste any time. I didn't expect to find you in the sack with somebody."

Ben and Linda exchanged smiling glances. "It just kind of happened," Linda said.

Ben had begun rubbing his hand down over Debbie's back and bottom, enjoying the smoothness of her skin. Linda reached up and playfully tugged Debbie's right nipple. She and Debbie looked into each others' eyes.

"Yeah, that was something else we talked about and never did," Debbie whispered. Ben's fingers found Debbie's pussy, marveling at its juiciness, and she leaned over and met Linda's lips. Ben watched the two women kiss, their passion obviously growing, with bemused wonderment. These last few days had been so full of surprises he was a little afraid to think what might happen next. Debbie's hand crept up his thigh and found his cock again, taking it gently this time.

Things seemed to flow in a dreamlike progression without any of them saying a word. Debbie was fingering Linda's pussy as well as holding his cock. And then she was licking Linda where her fingers had been, raising her butt in the air. An open invitation like this could only be answered with a readjustment of bodies and a slow insertion. Linda had her eyes closed but as he moved inside Debbie's drenched pussy he could see almost every sign of pleasure sweep across her face. He put his hands on Debbie's hips to pull her to him and she shook her ass as if to say, yes, I know you're there and I like what you're doing.

Linda went over first. He could sense Debbie's awareness of Linda's imminent orgasm and her intensified efforts to make it happen. Linda's hips bucked and she cried out as it hit her. He was second. Seeing and hearing Linda's pleasure was too much and he pulsed inside Debbie's cunt. He kept moving inside her although his enthusiasm had waned and was relieved to feel her fingers moving rapidly near his cock. Her head was resting on Linda's belly and her red hair blazed in the candlelight.

"Oh," she said. "Oh." Linda had recovered enough to begin fondling her breasts and that seemed to be enough to put her over. "Oh God yes. Oh yes. Jesus yes. I'm cumming boys and girls. Oh shit yes." He could feel her cunt tightening around him. And then there was stillness.

After a couple of long minutes he pulled out of her and, slowly drawing his right hand across her hip and back, collapsed beside Linda. Debbie, her head still resting on Linda's tummy, opened her eyes.

"Thanks," she said.

"You're welcome," he said. And fell asleep.

Sometime in the night he became dimly aware that Linda was returning the favor and slid back into sleep to the sound of Debbie's moans and sighs.

When he woke up in the morning he found his bare back pressed against Debbie's. He turned to look over Debbie's shoulder and could see that Linda was also lying on her side with her butt against Debbie's tummy. Debbie's arm was draped across Linda's belly. It was a sight that warmed the cockles of his woman loving heart. He eased out of bed and went to urinate. By the time Linda and Debbie woke up he'd made coffee and was working on breakfast.

"Oh shit," Debbie said. She wandered into the kitchen blinking. "I hope Ron doesn't shoot me."

"You have to tell him?" Linda asked, two steps behind her.

"Yep. Those're the rules. We've both been with other people a few times over the years but we always talked about it first."

"I'm impressed," Ben said. "A lot of people would figure what he doesn't know won't hurt him."

"But it would hurt me. And, eventually, it would hurt our relationship," Debbie said. "So it's the only way to go. Can we talk about something else?"

And so they did. After they'd eaten a leisurely breakfast on the patio Debbie said she had to be getting back home. Before she left she kissed them both.

"I'd love to do this again," she said. "If I survive."

"I don't know about Ben but I would. I seem to have acquired a new taste," Linda said, and she and Debbie exchanged a meaningful glance.

"Does a bear excrete in wooded areas?" Ben said.

In the laughter following this pungent phrase, Debbie drove

away.

"I got the definite impression that you enjoyed yourself," Linda said as they walked back to the cabin.

Ben hesitated before replying. "Yes, I did."

"Honey, I wasn't the least bit jealous if that's what you're worried about. Debbie and I used to fantasize about doing what we did last night. That was before she met Ron."

"You only talked?"

"Yeah. I think Debbie was ready to do more but I was too shy."

"So how did reality compare with your fantasies?"

They'd returned to the kitchen by this time. Ben poured himself another cup of coffee and sat next to Linda at the table.

"It was different," Linda said after a moment. "Felt more natural than I expected. But then I've known Debbie for a long time and I feel comfortable with you even though we met only a week ago."

"And you'd like to do it again?"

Linda's eyes met his with an unequivocal intensity. "Yes, I would."

Ben slipped his hand under her robe and squeezed her bare knee. "What did you like best about last night?" The look on her face told him she was becoming aroused.

"Living my fantasies," she said. "Living my fantasies with two people I like so much."

Ben's hand slid up her thigh. Her legs opened to accomodate him. His fingertips burrowed into the soft folds until they found the mouth of her cunt. "You're wet already," he said.

"I loved knowing you were fucking her when she was going down on me. You kept pushing her into me." Linda squirmed as Ben's fingers began rubbing her clit. Reaching out she felt the length of his erection through his jeans.

"And I loved watching you as I fucked her," he said. "Seeing how excited you were."

"I was thinking that I knew exactly how she felt, having your cock inside her."

"Did you like being with a woman for the first time?"

"Yeah, I did. It really wasn't the same as with a man. She was more gentle, teasing."

"Did you like going down on her?"

Linda's expression softened. "Oh yes."

"I'll have to taste her myself next time," Ben said. "We could do it together. Take turns."

"Damn," Linda said, "talking about last night is almost more exciting than being there."

"Yeah," Ben said, "sometimes the sharing afterward is the best part."

"I need you to fuck me, lover. Even if I am still kind of sore."

"That'll make two of us."

A short time later they were in bed, their bodies joined.

"Do you have any fantasies about what you'd like to do the next time?" He asked, looking into her eyes as he moved his cock inside her.

"Mmmmm," she said. "Lots of them. I want to lick her while you're fucking her. I want to watch. I want to kiss her while you're fucking me. Oh God! This is making me come."

He responded by wrapping his arms around her shoulders and thrusting powerfully.

"Oh yes. Fuck me lover," she moaned, lifting her hips to meet him. "Oh. Oh."

He could tell she was very close. He clutched her tighter and ground his belly against hers. It delighted him to feel the convulsive quivers as her body was overcome. The hot clenching of her cunt caused the deep thrilling pulsing of his own orgasm. They cried out in unison.

"Wow," she said after they'd held each other in silence for several minutes, "thinking about Debbie got me all fired up."

"What turned me on was feeling your excitement," he said.

"It amazes me how much at ease I am with you."

He pushed himself up with his arms, smiling down at her, and then shifted his body until he was lying on his back beside her. She cuddled close, resting her head on his chest. He put his arm around her shoulders. They lay together in a cozy silence.

"Well Babe," he said finally, "I need to head over to my place. I've got a bunch of things I have to do."

"I guess I kinda made a mess of your regular schedule."

"Yeah. But I'm not complaining."

"When will you be back?"

"In a day or two."

"I'm leaving Saturday to go back to Springfield."

"Okay. I'll be back before then. I promise."

After cuddling for awhile longer they got out of bed and he got dressed. They hugged and kissed on the patio and then she watched him walk down the path; just before he disappeared into the trees he turned and waved. She waved back. And then he was gone.

It felt strange knowing he wouldn't be back for a couple of days.

Once again she marveled at how much had changed in the last week. She was well aware that in many ways they were still essentially strangers but somehow, on an underlying emotional level, there was a real connection. She realized that even as she hoped that this would develop into an ongoing relationship her fears cautioned her not to let her expectations get too high.

As she entered the cabin she remembered the book she'd packed but hadn't had time for. This was a good time to get some reading done.

Linda awoke early on Friday, her last full day of freedom. The sun had already warmed the air and she'd kicked off the sheet sometime in her sleep. She lay in a half doze with the memories of the past ten days tumbling through her consciousness. It had exceeded her expectations a hundredfold. Her only regret was that her vacation was almost over, leaving a bittersweet feeling of uncertainty. Would Ben want to continue seeing her or would these wonderful memories turn out to be the only thing left to sustain her? She also felt some uneasiness about how this would effect her friendship with Debbie.

Opening her legs she touched herself. Most of the soreness was gone. She started to play with herself and then, smiling, stopped; it wasn't over yet. Ben had promised he'd be back and it was even possible that Debbie would return. She was aware of an increased flow of her juices at the mere thought of them.

Climbing out of bed she decided, with only a moment of hesitation, to remain naked. Something else she was going to miss. She wouldn't have much chance to indulge in the delightful feeling of being unencumbered by clothing with an inquisitive eleven year old boy popping in and out of the house without warning. Slipping a Bon Jovi CD into the player she went into the kitchen and began making her breakfast.

It was in the middle of the afternoon when she heard the crunch of tires on the gravel in the driveway. Still naked she peeked out the window and was thrilled to see Debbie's light blue Honda approaching. She opened the door and walked out on the porch.

"Well, I don't see any bullet holes in your forehead," Linda said as Debbie emerged from the car.

"Ron's cool," Debbie said. "He almost laughed his ass off when I told him I got caught peeking." She turned and snagged a bulging gym bag off the front seat. "He stopped laughing when I went on to say that I'd joined in. But after I finished telling him all the juicy details we had the best fuck we've had for a good long time."

"I was hoping it would work out."

"Yeah, me too." Their eyes met for a long moment. "Hey, I like your outfit. I think I'll go put mine on."

Linda stood in the bedroom doorway as Debbie undressed. "Ben left on Wednesday. He said he'd be back before I left," she said.

Debbie gave her an intent look. "You sound like you don't think he will."

"It's not that. But I really like him and I'm not sure what's going to happen after I leave here."

"Ah," Debbie said. "I hear you. He seems like a really nice guy."

"Nothing like the guys I usually get hooked up with. Is that what you're saying?"

Debbie laughed. "You've picked some doozies, it's true. But what makes you think Ben won't want to keep seeing you?"

"No reason, I'm just afraid he won't."

"I can understand that," Debbie said. "But there's only one way to find out. Time will tell."

"I know. I just hate being in suspense."

Debbie had gotten out of her clothes. "What do we do now?" She asked.

There was an awkward silence as they both thought the same thing but neither had the courage to say it out loud.

"We could listen to music," Linda said. "Go for a walk. You know the list as well as I do."

"A walk would be nice. It's been awhile since I've spent time out here."

After putting on their shoes they started down the path into the woods. Both were hoping that they'd run into Ben along the way but he never appeared. Linda showed Debbie the pool where she and Ben had met and told her the whole story. They enjoyed the cool water for awhile, and talked. They were both relieved to discover that their friendship hadn't been affected by the sudden inclusion of open sex. It was almost evening when they got back to the cabin.

"You have a visitor," Debbie said, pointing out the red Nissan pickup truck parked next to her Honda.

"Oh shit!" Linda said.

"Maybe it's Ben."

Linda was surprised to realize that she'd never thought of Ben as owning a vehicle. To her he was the man who'd materialized out of the woods.

"Oh my, naked wood nymphs," said a voice from the shadows of the patio. "This must be my luck day." Linda recognized Ben's voice.

"Kinda overdressed, aren't you?" Debbie said as they got close enough to see him wearing shorts and a t-shirt.

"That's easily remedied," Ben said, standing up and pulling his t-shirt over his head. Then his shorts fell. They saw that he was half erect.

"I've missed you Babe," he said, drawing Linda into a tight embrace.

"I'll let you lovebirds get reacquainted," Debbie said with a laugh. "I'll go see what there is to eat."

When they entered the kitchen several minutes later she was laying out the ingredients for sandwiches.

"I take it Don didn't get too upset about our little adventure," Ben said.

"Ron," the two women said, almost simultaneously.

"Ron. Sorry."

"He was a little freaked at first," Debbie said. "But in the end it turned him on. I think he's hoping for another hot story when I get back."

"Is there going to be one?" Ben asked with studied nonchalance.

Debbie glanced at Linda.

"I certainly hope so," Linda said.

They all laughed at the sudden relaxation of tension.

"I guess that answers that question," Debbie said. "Linda and I have been kind of dancing around it since I got here."

They made sandwiches, poured something to drink, and carried them out to the patio. Now that they'd determined what was going to happen later the conversation flowed smoothly. Mostly they shared what they'd been doing since Wednesday. Linda, who'd primarily read and listened to music, was soon finished with her account. Ben took longer because he'd had to explain the rudiments of the business he conducted over the Internet. When it was Debbie's turn she described how she'd broken the news of their threesome to Ron and his reactions. In explicit detail. By the time she was finished they were all ready for the next stage.

"Shall we adjourn to the bedroom, ladies?" Ben said. Without a word Linda and Debbie gathered their dishes and went inside. Ben quickly followed.

Together they lit the candles. Linda was the first to get into bed. Ben and Debbie soon joined her.

"Now what?" Linda said.

"I thought you had some pretty good ideas the other afternoon," Ben said, snuggling up to her and running his hand over her tummy till he found a breast.

"Oh, do tell," Debbie said.

"You've put me on the spot."

"There isn't a wet spot yet," Debbie said. "We're working on that." She moved in closer and began sucking on Linda's other nipple.

"You wanted to watch Debbie and me together."

"I feel silly," Linda said.

"Please don't," Debbie said. "I loved watching Ben fucking you. That's how all this got started. Remember?" She gently pushed Linda's legs apart with her hand and then insinuated the tips of her fingers until she found the mouth of Linda's cunt. She winked at Ben as she encountered silky wetness.

"You wanted to lick her while I was fucking her," Ben said, smiling at Linda's embarrassment.

"Damn!" Debbie said. "This is making me hot."

"And you wanted her to kiss you while you and I were fucking."

"I'm sure not going to forget how good your memory is," Linda said. "See if I tell you anything again."

Ben laughed.

"Hey, that all sounds good to me," Debbie said. "Let's do it."

"Ahhh," Linda sighed, closing her eyes as the head of Ben's cock slid into her.

"I'm going to lick you first and then I'm going to kiss you," Debbie said. Ben leaned back so she could get in between them.

"Ohhh," was Linda's response as Debbie acted on the first part of her statement.

Ben reached down and cupped Debbie's breast, tugging her nipple between his fingers, as he moved slowly back and forth. He could feel Debbie's tongue flick across the shaft of his cock and her hair brushing against his belly. He watched as Linda's hand reached out and stroked the curve of Debbie's ass before easing further down and out of sight. Judging from Debbie's wiggles and sighs Linda's fingers had discovered a sensitive spot.

"Ummmm," Linda said as Debbie turned her attention to the second part of her assertion, covering Linda's mouth with her own.

Ben quickly realized that this change in position put Debbie's pussy within his reach. He felt her velvet warmth envelop two of his fingers. Pressing them in to the knuckles he twisted his hand. Debbie moaned and pushed back. Her wetness excited him. Withdrawing from Linda he got behind Debbie and replaced his fingers with his cock. Linda rolled until she was lying on her side, watching them in the flickering candlelight. He could see her right hand bobbing in her crotch.

"Do you like watching us?" He asked.

"Mmmmm," Linda said. "I've never seen people have sex before in real life. Only videos."

"Didn't you see us the first time?" Debbie said.

"I had my eyes closed," Linda said. "And by the time I opened them you were done."

Debbie laughed. "Is there anything special you want us to do?"

Linda hesitated. "I'd like to see. Ummm. Him inside you."

Debbie crawled forward, leaving Ben's cock cooling in the air behind her. Seconds later she was lying on her side, her head pointed towards Linda's feet and her pussy an arm's length away from Linda's face.

"Put it in honey," she said, lifting her leg into the air.

Ben scooted up against her bottom and pushed his cock between her legs. She guided him in.

"How does it look?" Debbie asked, watching Linda's face.

"Looks great," Linda said, her eyes fixed on the sight. "How does it feel?"

"Mmmmmm," Debbie said.

Linda extended her arm, ran her fingertips through Debbie's red fluff, down the pink groove, along the length of Ben's cock, and then cupped his balls.

"Oh shit!" Ben said. He gripped Debbie's shoulders with his hands to increase his leverage and began thrusting harder.

"Yeah. Fuck her lover," Linda said. "Make her cum."

"Oh, oh," Debbie moaned. "God that feels good."

Linda bridged the distance between them and began running her tongue slowly up and down the length of Debbie's open pussy, sucking her clit, and licking Ben's rapidly moving cock. Debbie started finger fucking her friend's cunt. They were all making guttural sounds of pleasure now.

"Oh shit, I'm so close," Debbie said.

"Oh yeah," Ben groaned, never slackening.

Linda was squirming convulsively on Debbie's busy fingers. She now had three of them inside her. She sucked hungrily at Debbie's pussy, feeling Ben's cock sliding against her nose.

"Unhh," Ben moaned, quivering. Seconds later Linda tasted his cum mixed with Debbie's juices.

"Oh yes. Oh shit yes," Debbie sighed.

With Debbie's fingers still inside her Linda began rubbing her clit vigorously. Closing her eyes, smelling the musky scents in front of her, she replayed the whole scene in her mind. Soon she too shuddered with orgasm.

There was a period of sated silence. Finally Linda got up and went to the bathroom. When she came out she snuggled up to Ben's back and reached over him to put her hand on Debbie's shoulder. They lay quietly for another couple of minutes.

"I don't know about you ladies but I enjoyed the hell out of that," Ben said. Both women laughed.

Then, after Ben complained of an arm that was half asleep, they rearranged themselves so they were all lying on their backs with Ben in the middle. Linda and Debbie rested their heads on Ben's chest; he put his arms around their shoulders. They talked quietly.

As they talked they touched each other. Soft sensual caresses. At first it was simply for the pleasure of contact but slowly, once they'd rested, it became more heated. Linda ran her hand over Ben's belly and closed it around his soft cock. Debbie lifted her head and kissed him. He cupped a breast in each hand, playing with both their nipples.

"Oh yeah," Linda said as Ben's cock began to swell. She moved down and took him in her mouth.

"That looks good," Debbie said, breaking off the kiss to watch. Sitting up she began to tease his balls with her fingers. With a slurp Linda pulled her mouth off Ben's now fully erect cock and pointed it toward her friend. "Mmmmm," Debbie said, taking her turn.

Linda lay down on her back perpendicular to Ben's body, putting her legs over him, opening herself. "Fuck me lover," she said. Ben turned over on his side and Debbie guided his cock into Linda's ripe cunt. "Oh God," Linda sighed as she felt him probe snugly into her depths.

Debbie leaned over, her breasts pressed against Ben's hip, feeling his muscles tighten and relax as he moved back and forth, and flicked Linda's clit with the tip of her tongue. She rubbed her hands over Linda's thighs and belly before closing them around her breasts, pulling at her hard nipples. For a time they were all absorbed in the easy flow of pleasure they were sharing; in the soft cocooning glow of the candles there were only the quiet sounds of skin against skin, squishy wetness, and deep sighs and moans.

"Oh yeah. Oh yeah. I'm going to come," Linda groaned at last. Ben moved faster and Debbie sucked her clit more fervently. "Oh God. That feels so good." She frantically bucked against them as she felt her climax beginning. "Yeah. Oh yeah. That's it. That's it."

Debbie, aroused by the intensity of her friend's excitement, plunged her fingers into her own pussy.

Then they both felt Linda's body clenching with orgasm.

"Oh yeah, Babe, oh yeah," Ben said as he felt her cunt tighten around his cock. The squeezing stimulation triggered his own orgasm. Giving an incoherent shout he felt his semen pulsing into her.

Moments later Debbie was joining them, giving voice to the deep sensations that shook her body.

"Oh Jesus, it just seems to get better," Ben said, after a period of rest.

"Mmmm," Debbie said.

Linda had fallen asleep.

The next morning they were all in a solemn mood. Ben and Debbie took their cue from Linda who was coming to terms with the knowledge that her vacation was very nearly over.

"I don't know if I'm ready to face real life again," Linda said as they ate breakfast.

"I know what you mean," Debbie said.

"Sometimes it seems to me that this is real life and the other isn't," Ben said.

Linda and Debbie turned to him, their expressions doubtful.

"And I *was* hoping we could do this some more," he added. "I'd like to visit you in Springfield, if that would be okay."

Linda looked at Ben as if she didn't believe her ears. Debbie smiled as she gazed at Linda.

"I'd like that," Linda said.

"Maybe we could make it a foursome," Debbie said. "Ron confessed the other night that he's always hankered to get in your knickers."

Linda looked shocked.

"Just a thought," Debbie said.

"No, no, I'd be willing," Linda said. "It's just that I never imagined he found me attractive."

"Well he does. Very." Debbie said.

"Oh my," Linda said.

As soon as they finished their breakfast Debbie got her things together and put them in her car. Just before she climbed in they all exchanged hugs and kisses.

"I'd better get going myself," Ben said as soon as Debbie's car had disappeared down the drive. As he collected his things Linda wrote her address and phone number on a piece of paper, handing it to him when he was ready to leave. He gave her one of his business cards.

They hugged and kissed for a long time.

"I'll be seeing you Babe," he said. "I promise. I really like the way we are together."

Linda had tears in her eyes as she watched his truck move down the driveway. Then she turned towards the cabin to start packing her things.

The hawk drifted over the empty cabin, moving west. His sharp eyes could see the trees that shaded the quiet pool where once he'd seen the joining of two naked human bodies. But this didn't even enter his consciousness. The mouse scuttling through the grass in the meadow beyond was much more interesting.

Royally Fucked

He was the one who wasn't trying to jump every woman in the Grownup Fun Finder New England chatroom. He didn't say much but when he did it was to the point and from the heart. It was clear from his handle, blknsweet, that he was a black man. For some reason I'd been thinking about black men. A lot. It kind of put me off, though, that he'd say he tasted sweet. How did he know? Had he tasted himself?

But on a whim I clicked on his handle to look at his profile. I quickly realized that he was talking about his personality and not something else when he said he was sweet. And he did seem to be. His profile gave me the same feeling I had about him in the chatroom. Okay. I'll admit it. The next thing I checked was his "male endowment". So sue me.

He said he was of average length but "extra thick". I felt myself tingle down there. So where does he live? Oh shit. My heart started beating fast. He lives in Albany. I sat back in my chair and exhaled nervously. The palms of my hands were damp. I knew I was going to do something that, if I thought about it too long, would scare me to death.

"Hey blknsweet, we're neighbors," I typed.

"Is that so," he replied.

"I live in Albany too."

"Cool. Would you like to meet sometime?"

"Maybe. Let's get to know each other a little first."

"That's cool. Do you have Yahoo Messenger?"

"Yes."

"Contact me. The handle's the same."

And I did. Even though it took me a couple of minutes to type in his handle because my hands were shaking so much. He responded right away and we began to chat. With a gentle calmness he steered the conversation, asking me questions and offering information about himself. And he seemed to want to know me as a person. The subject of sex was only touched on briefly. The more we chatted the more I felt myself relaxing. He told me his name was Royal. I told him mine.

We chatted often over the next several weeks. The subject of sex was coming up more and more and we were both enjoying the flirtation. He asked if I'd like to see a nude photo of him. I said, "But of course." God, he was beautiful. Rich dark brown skin and the build of an athlete. He told me that he'd been a wrestler in college and had made a point of keeping in shape afterwards. It made me feel very insecure; I mean, why would he want to be with me? I'm 45 and time has done some damage. And I could lose a few pounds. But a girl can dream. The only disappointment was that he was soft. When I said so he replied by saying that he wanted to keep some secrets for when we met.

He asked for a photo of me and I kept putting him off. But he kept asking. So one Saturday when everyone was out of the house I figured out how to use my husband's digital camera and started taking some pictures of myself using the timer feature the camera had. I started out full clothed. I knew, however, that he wanted more than that. I slipped out of my dress and took one of myself in my bra and panties. I felt like some kind of pervert. But I was having fun. I took off my bra and cupped my breasts in my hands, thinking of him seeing me like this. I could feel the familiar ache of excitement in my pussy. The last photo was of me on the bed, wide open, showing him everything I had. I had to use my vibrator. A couple of times.

The photo I sent him only showed my face. He said he thought I was beautiful. I didn't really believe him but there was a little spark of hope that seemed to grow stronger every day. I'd look at the photo of him lying on his side on a bed, smiling into the camera as if looking into my eyes, his penis and balls dangling against his thigh, and try to imagine what it would be like to be with him.

He asked me if I had any special fantasies. After sharing a couple of rather tame ideas, and with some prodding from him, I confessed that I'd never been with a black man. He asked if there was anything else. It took me a couple of days to work up the courage to tell him I had fantasies of being with two men at once. He revealed that he'd been in quite a few threesomes with a woman and another guy and had enjoyed them. Immensely.

I very shyly told him he was sending me to my bed to use my

vibrator on myself after every chat session. He said he liked thinking about that. He kept asking me if I was ready to meet and each time I told him I wasn't. But the flames of hope and desire were burning brighter . He would sign off by saying he was a patient man. And he was.

"Lena," he wrote, finally. "How about getting together for a cup of coffee? No expectations. No pressure."

I took a deep breath. "Okay." I could feel myself trembling as we made the plans.

We agreed to meet at a Starbucks in a mall not far from my house in three days, in the evening; I figured I'd say I needed to do some grocery shopping. As the time of our meeting drew near I became more and more nervous. By the morning of the fateful day I was a wreck. What am I doing? I thought to myself. Meeting a strange man for sex. A gorgeous younger black man. With a well upholstered middle-aged body like mine. I'm insane.

I almost didn't go. I got myself there in stages. I'll just go to the mall, I told myself. I won't meet him. Once I was at the mall I decided I'd walk past Starbucks, I wouldn't go in. Maybe I'd catch a glimpse of him. My knees were shaking so hard I could barely walk. I felt as if I was losing the sensation in my legs. The first time I cruised by my heart sank. He wasn't there. Two black guys were sitting at one of the tables but all the single men were white. Several stores past Starbucks I sank down onto a bench, my hands clasped between my thighs, biting my lip. I must have looked odd but I was past caring. After sort of pulling myself together I made a pact with myself that I'd give it one more shot and then go home. There still weren't any single black men. But when I was almost past, almost free, one of the two black men seated together caught my eye. I realized it was Royal. I stopped, frozen. He smiled and beckoned me over.

"This is Nathan," Royal said, once I'd managed to cross the distance between the entry way and their table. He stood up to pull out a chair and help me get seated. I needed help. "I hope I wasn't out of line to invite him. I was thinking of your fantasy. He's a nice guy too."

I looked at Nathan. Thinking he must know I had fantasies about being fucked by two men. I knew I was blushing. I was probably the color of a firetruck. He looked into my eyes and smiled, as if a woman wanting to be with two men was the most natural thing in the world. He wasn't leering at me at all. He was a good looking man, darker than Royal, and much slimmer. Not skinny, by any means, but not as built up.

While Royal went to the counter to get me a Caffe Latte, Nathan and I began to talk. He asked me some general questions and I struggled to answer coherently. But Royal was right, he was a nice guy. After Royal returned the three of us chatted. I began to relax. And then I started having fun. They were both warm and funny.

Nathan was quieter and in some ways I felt closer to him. But Royal had a sexual aura that made my body hum. The sound of Royal's voice, deep and resonate, caused a vibration deep inside me.

The reason for our meeting wasn't brought up until the end.

"Well, as far as I'm concerned you're a beautiful woman, as I've mentioned. I'd love to be with you," Royal said. "I think Nathan will agree."

"Oh yeah," Nathan said. I was stunned by the sincere appreciation in his voice.

I took a deep breath. "If you want me you can have me," I said. I couldn't believe I was saying this. But I'd never meant anything more in my life.

"Great," Royal said, standing up. "I promised not to pressure you so let's leave it at that for now. If you still feel the same way in a couple of days we'll set something up. Come on, we'll walk you to your car."

Nathan stood and I did too. It felt strange to be escorted by two lovely men who I knew desired me. Part of me hoped that no one I knew would see me and another part wanted the whole world to notice. We walked through the parking lot and I realized they were both wearing Lagerfeld cologne. One more thing to stoke my fires. As if I needed anything.

"This was fun," Royal said when we got to my soccer mom SUV. "You're exactly the person I thought you'd be."

I was staggered by his compliment. And I was beginning to believe him. I offered no resistance when he pulled me close, his full lips melting over mine. His tongue teased. I opened my mouth and sucked him in. He pressed his hips against my tummy and I could feel him hardening. I slid my hands around his waist and pulled him closer. I could feel him chuckling into my mouth. Sliding my right hand down I felt the bulge between us. He hadn't been kidding about how thick he was. It almost felt as big around as a soda can. I grasped him in my fingers and he pressed against me. I was moaning. And then he stepped back.

I felt bereft. The car door was cold against my bottom. Royal took hold of my elbow and gently guided me towards Nathan. I knew he wasn't forcing me, that if I hadn't wanted to he would have stopped. But God did I want to. A moment later it was

Nathan's arms and Nathan's lips. This man, having just watched me with Royal, was already hard. I could tell he wasn't as thick but he seemed longer. By the time he let me go I knew my panties were drenched. This was like a dream.

"Goodnight Lena," Royal said. I shakily got into my car.

"Goodnight Lena," Nathan said, just before I closed the door.

I watched them walk away. I thought about feeling their cocks. And their kisses. I pulled up my dress and got myself off. I had to stop again before I got home and do it again. This lady was going to get fucked. Oh boy, was she going to get fucked. By two beautiful black men. I had to stop once more.

I chatted with Royal the next day and we began to make plans. He said he could meet with me alone or with Nathan. I said I wanted both of them.

"Yeah, I kinda thought you would," he wrote. "I could tell how turned on you were."

"I had to masturbate three times before I got home and then lock myself in the bathroom." Sharing this kind of thing was getting easier all the time.

"Lol, lol, lol. You're a very sensual woman, Lena. That's what I like about you. Nathan likes that too. We're gonna love getting you all hot and juicy and fucking you until none of us can fuck anymore."

Oh God, talk about hot and juicy. I felt myself starting to flow.

It took almost two weeks before we could make any definite plans. And then it just seemed to work out. The girls wanted to go to a concert in Buffalo and my husband insisted on taking them because he didn't trust their friends. Because the concert would end late in the evening he decided that they'd stay in a motel before coming back the next day. It was easy enough for me to say I had too much to do at home to spend two days away. It turned out that both Royal and Nathan could make it at the same time. I was very excited and more than a little scared. I kept hopping around like a demented rabbit. And couldn't keep my hands off my pussy. It was kind of embarrassing to have to go out at 10:30 at night to get batteries for my vibrator. My husband and kids noticed my agitation but I told them I was worried about something at work. None of them seemed to question my answer.

A minute after I waved goodbye to my family, late in the afternoon, I was in the shower. I primped and pampered myself. Put on makeup. Did my nails, on my toes as well as my fingers. Sprayed on perfume. And then I put on lingerie. And took off lingerie. And tried on one dress. Then tried on another. And tried not to think that in a very short time I was going to be doing unspeakable things with two men in my very own bedroom.

I was in my short robe, with nothing on underneath, when I heard the sound of two car doors slamming. I ran to the window. Oh God, it was them. The doorbell rang. I stood in the foyer for what seemed like forever, breathing heavily, and then opened the door. The first thing I saw was Royal's broad smile as he walked inside. Nathan was right behind him.

"You ready for us, Baby?" Royal said. He seemed to know how nervous I was.

"As much as I'll ever be," I said, my voice cracking.

Royal scooped me up in his arms and kissed me, covering my mouth with those warm full lips. I could feel Nathan's hand slipping up under the robe and touching my bare bottom. Royal cupped the back of my head, running his fingers into my short brown hair, and eased his tongue between my lips. I could hear myself moaning. Nathan's fingers found my pussy.

"This girl is more than ready," Nathan said, stirring his fingers inside me. "I think it's time to adjourn to the bedroom."

They each took one of my hands and I led them down the hall and into the bedroom.

"I think you should undress us," Royal said. "Go ahead, have fun with it."

I began by unbuttoning his shirt. When I was finished I pulled his shirt out of his pants and ran my hands over his chest and sides. He was so solid. I licked his nipples and drew in the familiar scent of his cologne. I pulled the shirt down his arms. My fingers were trembling as I undid his belt, and opened his fly. I pushed his pants down his legs. Now there were only a pair of red boxer shorts. I pushed those down too.

"Oh," I breathed as his cock was revealed. It was very thick. And hard. I tried to put my hands around it, my small white hands. I saw a bead of precum on the tip and bent down to lick it up. Royal sighed.

"Do Nathan," he said, his hands on my shoulders, pushing me back.

I was aware that Royal was taking off his shoes and stepping out of his pants while I performed the undressing process on Nathan. The moment I was done I felt Royal's hands tugging at my robe. All at once the three of us were as naked as the day we'd been born.

"Come on Babe," Royal said, climbing into bed. I followed. Nathan was right behind. There I was, snuggled between these two beautiful men, their hard cocks brushing my thighs. Then they each grabbed a leg and pulled me open.

Everything that happened next is kind of a blur in my memory. A blur filled with indescribable physical pleasure. I'll try to remember it all as clearly as I can.

I think it was Royal who had his fingers in my pussy next. And on my clit. Rubbing me. I reached out to take their hard cocks in each of my hands. At the same moment they each leaned over to suck and lick my nipples. I'd never experienced anything remotely like it. The mere idea of it made me gaga. To have two beautiful men wanting me, the proof was in my hands, was enough to make a girl come right there. And to have them giving my breasts such sweet attention, hearing the moist sounds, seeing their faces and pink tongues, feeling my sensitive titties responding, put me right over the edge. It seemed as of from then on I was having one orgasm after another.

Royal was working two of his fingers, slick with my pussy juice, into my bottom. I'd told him I liked that. He was gentle and careful and I felt myself relax. They slid right in. He began moving them in and out, twisting them slightly. It felt marvelous. Then he pressed his large thumb deep inside my cunt. It didn't feel like a pussy now. It was definitely a cunt, all hot and hungry. He was fingerfucking me in both my holes.

"Feel good, Baby?" He said.

"Oh God yes." I moaned. "Don't stop."

Nathan lifted his head and looked down to watch Royal's busy fingers. Then he looked up to catch my eyes. He seemed to enjoy the expression of pleasure on my face. And then he repositioned himself and began licking my clit. He used one of his hands to play with my breasts. I thought I was going to die. I'd never been so excited in my life.

I think I came at least twice before Royal pulled out his fingers and stretched out beside me. Nathan was still eating me.

"Would you like to ride me, Baby?" Royal said, holding his thick hard cock straight up. I didn't need a second invitation. I straddled Royal, facing him. I looked down to watch the big, chocolate colored, head swallowed by the pink lips of my cunt. I slid down a bit and then lifted up. He felt so good inside me. I could see my juices gleaming on his shaft. I pushed down again, taking more this time. I felt so full.

Royal was playing with my swinging breasts while Nathan, behind me, was running his hands over my body. Over my bottom and back, caressing me.

"You're so soft, Lena," Nathan said. "I love the feel of your skin."

"And I love the way you're touching me," I said, turning to look at him.

Royal was starting to thrust up into me, groaning a little. His sounds excited me. Nathan was fingering my butthole.

"Put it in, Nathan," I said. I meant his finger.

He moved up behind me and I felt his cock pushing at my behind.

"Wait. Wait." I yelped. "I'm not sure I'm ready for that."

He backed away slightly. Royal stopped moving.

"I'm won't hurt you, Lena," Nathan said. "If it hurts I'll stop."

I did want him to do it. "Okay," I said.

"Hang on, I brought some lube," Nathan said. He got off the bed and went to his pants. Royal and I resumed fucking . I closed my eyes and moved on him. I was thinking about how it was going to feel to have them both inside me.

In no time at all, it seemed, Nathan was back. He drizzled the lube on my bottom and began working on my hole with his fingers. He was as gentle as Royal had been and soon I was relaxed again. And then it was his cock slowly pushing its way in.

"Oh. Oh. That feels so good," I said. It was very exciting to feel them both moving inside me. My moans spurred them on and they both began thrusting powerfully. It was kind of awkward but satisfying in a way I'd never known.

"I'm coming, Lena," Nathan said with a groan, sliding deep inside me and going rigid. And then I could feel him pulsing.

"Oh yeah, oh yeah," Royal said. "Me too, here it comes Baby."

And I could feel him too. I shuddered with my own orgasm.

I sank onto Royal's chest, squashing my breasts against him. Nathan remained inside me but supported himself on his arms so his full weight wouldn't be on me. Then he withdrew.

"Well, now you can say you've been royally fucked," Royal said. He gently eased me over onto my back.

"Oh Jesus Royal," Nathan said. He got off the bed and headed for the bathroom, "I think it's about time you put that one on the shelf and left it there."

"But it's true," I said. Royal put his hand on my belly, sliding up to my breast. We could hear Nathan urinating, the toilet flushing, and then the water faucet came on. When it was quiet I said, "but I got Nathanly fucked too." We heard him laugh, the sound booming against the tiles.

"It doesn't have quite the same ring," he said, emerging from the bathroom, his cock and balls damp. He climbed into bed with us. His hand was soon on my other breast. Royal got up to make his own trip to the bathroom, quickly returning.

We cuddled, stroking and caressing each other. The guys didn't try to touch but they didn't seem to mind if their hands made contact from time to time. It was almost non-sexual. More the human comfort of skin against skin. I felt very relaxed and cared for.

"How long have you known each other?" I asked.

"Since we were kids," Royal said.

"I take it I'm not the first woman you've both done this with?" I wasn't sure why I asked this. A part of me knew I didn't want to know the answer.

"No, you're not," Royal said, turning to look me in the eyes. "Does that bother you?"

"A little," I said. It was a lot more than a little but I wasn't going to say so.

Nathan picked up on my feelings. "We don't team up on every woman who crosses our path," he said. "There've been three over the years. You're the fourth."

"And you're special, as they were. I had that sense about you when we chatted and Nathan agreed when we met at the mall," Royal said.

During this conversation they were running their hands over my body and I was running mine over both of theirs. Gently exploring.

"The last one was five years ago," Nathan said.

"White?" I asked.

"Black," Royal said. "We're equal opportunity fuckers." We all laughed.

"What happened?" I asked.

"Her life changed. She wanted to find something more traditional. We see her sometimes at church," Nathan said.

"At church?" I said. I had difficulty envisioning the two of them in a church. Any church I'd been in, anyway.

"Yeah," Nathan said, smiling. "She sings in the choir. We're the ones who don't show up that often. But Royal and I were raised in the church. She's always friendly but it's obvious she wants to leave those times we had behind."

"The other two were white," Royal said. "But that was way back when. They're long gone."

The conversation continued, jumping from topic to topic as conversations do. Then, slowly, the gentle exploration became more heated. Nathan began playing with my pussy, slipping two of his large fingers deep into my cunt. Royal shifted around so that I could take his half hard cock in my mouth. I enjoyed feeling it

82

swell between my lips. But soon the size of it made my jaws ache so I contented myself with licking the shaft and kissing and sucking the head.

Nathan moved into position between my legs and began teasing the lips of my pussy with the head of his cock. Sometimes entering me an inch or so and then pulling out. He was beginning to drive me crazy.

"Fuck me Nathan," I moaned. "I need you inside me."

He pushed himself all the way in and then started fucking me with long gentle strokes. Our conversation had created an intimate bond among the three of us and now it felt more like making love. Royal moved so that I could rest my head on his thigh, playing with my hair. I continued to stroke his cock. The physical sensations were delicious but having this sense of glowing intimacy amplified my pleasure ten-fold.

I could look into Nathan's eyes, reading the desire he felt for me, and then turn my head and look into Royal's. Nathan was moving faster now. He and I were beginning to express the intensity of our feelings with moans and sighs.

"Oh God, Nathan, you're going to make me come," I said.

"Yeah, Baby, come for me. Tell me how it feels," he grunted.

"Oh God, it feels fantastic," I said, "I love the way you fuck me."

"Shit you two look beautiful," Royal said. "Get that sweet cunt all warmed up for me, Nate."

"Oh, yeah, I want your big cock in me next," I moaned. "That big black dick filling me up. Oh shit. Fuck me Nathan. Oh sweetheart." And I was gone. Warm flowing waves of orgasm washed over my body. The power of it made me quiver and shake. Then Nathan was coming too.

We all rested there for awhile, quiet and relaxed. Royal kept running his fingers through my hair, touching me, caressing my skin. And then at last Nathan pushed himself up and lay down next to me. Royal shifted his thigh out from under my head, replacing it with a pillow, and moved over the other side. He guided me so that my bottom was towards him.

"My pussy's kind of sore," I said. "It doesn't often get this much attention."

"Okay, I'd love to fuck you but I don't need to," Royal said.

"Oh no, I want you. Just go easy."

"Mmmmm. A greedy girl," Royal said.

"Yeah, that's me. God I'm loving this."

Royal eased himself into me, stretching the walls of my cunt. There was a little stinging pain but as the song says, it hurt so good. Nathan moved closer and began kissing me while his hand played with my breasts, teasing the nipples. Royal was so gentle and sweet. I felt as if I was swimming in a warm pool of sensuality. This went on and on. For what seemed like hours. A slow liquid flow like honey in the sun. Then I felt Royal getting tense. He kept the same pace but it was obvious he was close. And then he was pulsing into me. Groaning with pleasure. I didn't come again but I didn't need to. And once again we were all resting, spent and relaxed. Drifting into sleep.

I woke up to find that the first signs of daylight were showing in the windows. Nathan's sleeping face was right in front of me. And I could feel Royal's body pressed against my backside. I was cradled between them. I lay there trying to absorb all that had happened in the last ten hours. I became aware of Royal's hand sliding over my hip. And then his cock swelling against my thigh.

"I'm sorry, honey," I whispered. "My cunt's way too sore."

"That's cool," he whispered back, "I like touching you."

We lay in a half doze and the light grew stronger. I wanted to purr as his hands explored me. I reached out and touched Nathan, smiling. His eyes opened sleepily.

"Morning," Nathan said. And then he was touching me too.

"I suppose we'd better get going," Royal said, after awhile. He got out of bed and started dressing. Then Nathan did too. I lay in bed, watching them. When they were ready to go I got up and they each took one of my hands. We walked down the hallway to the door.

"Think you'd like to do this again sometime?" Royal asked.

I snorted. Not a very feminine sound, I know, but that's what it was. "Are you kidding? If you guys want me I sure as hell want you."

"Oh, we want you," Nathan said, pulling me into his arms and giving me a long sweet kiss.

"And if you decide you like one of us better than the other, that's okay too," Royal said, taking his turn.

"No, I think I could get addicted to being with two guys at once," I said, as soon as he'd released me.

"We'll be in touch then," Royal said.

I hid behind the door as they departed and then closed it behind them. I walked back to the bedroom, feeling the aching soreness in my crotch. It felt so good. I snuggled into the sheets, smelling the powerful scent of my two beautiful men. Rubbed my naked body against the soft texture. And fell asleep.

Needafriend Finds Friend4u

She couldn't remember the first time she saw him. It seemed that he'd been around for awhile, living in the apartment building next door to hers. A glimpse of motion, a car in the street with a face in profile framed by the window, a voice calling out a daughter's name were only formless memories.

But the first time she became aware of him was like seeing a color photo after years spent looking at grainy black and white images in newsprint. She could recall the moment with perfect clarity. She'd been standing, looking out her window, when he walked out of his apartment and went to the mailboxes that were situated on the side of the building. There was no reason, that she could discern, why this moment would be different. But it was. She found herself liking the way he moved. Relaxed but with a gentle power, at home in his body. She watched until he returned to his apartment and disappeared inside. And knew she had to watch him again.

It was strange. It made her feel like a voyeur. But she couldn't help herself. It became a secret source of sustenance. Much like the friendships she'd started making through her computer. The ones her husband sort of knew about but didn't pay any attention to.

And then watching wasn't enough. She began taking the dogs out for their walk at the times she knew he might be outside. And they started to say hello to each other, smiling, nodding, giving friendly waves. She liked his face. He seemed open, friendly, and direct.

For several weeks she didn't think about why this was happening. And then she became aware of what her body was telling her. She realized that seeing him aroused her. Not fiery passion and drenching wetness. But it was there. And it was growing.

And then one day, while she was out with the dogs, he and his daughter came walking towards her, apparently on their way back from the convenience store. They'd never met like this before and it made her a little nervous. Not fearful, but restless with anticipation. He stopped when they were a few feet apart. She did too.

"Hi, I'm Roger," he said. She responded to his warm open smile with one of her own. "I think it's about time we introduced ourselves since we see so much of each other. This is my daughter Amy."

"Hi Roger. I'm Ella. Hi Amy." The little girl smiled shyly.

"See you around then," he said, and he and Amy moved on.

But now there were snatches of conversation. About the weather, references to activities planned for the day. There was also a faint undercurrent of tension. She wondered if he felt it too.

ROGER SAT AT HIS COMPUTER looking through profiles on the Grownup Fun Finder personals site. His divorce had been final for over two years now and he hadn't been with a woman in all that time. For many months he hadn't even thought about it; it was too painful. The divorce had been brutal and the emotional wounds had taken a long time to heal. He wasn't sure they had healed, even now.

But he was beginning to want someone. Not something very serious, maybe. A friend. Someone to hold. Laughter. He missed simply lying in bed with a woman, both of them naked, sharing an intimate laugh. So he'd started looking around on the Internet. GFF seemed like a good place to start because a lot of the women, as far as he could tell, were looking for the same thing he was. The only problem was that most of the local women he contacted either didn't reply or stopped writing after a couple of emails. He had met two women face to face but the chemistry wasn't there.

He'd made several long distance friends and discovered he enjoyed cybersex. It wasn't the real thing but it sure beat masturbating alone. It was nice to share the experience. One of his friends had shown him the excitement of a webcam and he'd bought one so he could join her. They'd been having a lot of fun together.

The thing was, though, there was someone he had his eye on. Ella, the woman in the apartment building next to his. But she might as well be as far away as his long distance friends. He didn't know what her situation was. The likelihood that she'd want the kind of no strings relationship that he was looking for seemed infinitesimal. And he wasn't the kind of guy to take a shot at it just to see if he could get some, to Hell with the consequences. For one thing it hurt too much to be turned down.

But he sure did like her. Couldn't say what it was. But there was a glow that seemed to radiate from her that warmed his heart. Lifted his spirits. It had begun to mean a lot to him that they seemed to see each other at least once a day. The days they didn't were dull and dreary, no matter how brightly the sun was shining. He liked her body. He'd always liked full figured women, so soft and warm and full of mystery. With a thin woman it was pretty much all out there and the mystery was gone. But exploring a big woman's body, oh shit, thinking like this would only drive him crazy. Ella wasn't interested in him. He tried to connect with his webcam pal but she didn't respond.

ELLA WAS LYING IN BED with the covers pushed back. Her husband had been gone when she'd awakened. She tried to figure out what time it was from the angle of the sun coming in the windows but soon gave up. It was Sunday morning and the time wasn't important. She pulled up her nightdress and spread her legs halfway open. Sweet tinglings of arousal flowed through her body. It felt good to lie open this way in the sunlight. She thought about going into the bathroom and getting the foot thingie she used like a vibrator but it seemed like too much effort. Her hand slid down and she touched herself with the tips of her fingers. Candy had begun to ooze lubrication.

Roger entered her thoughts with that easy powerful walk he had. She tried to imagine what it would be like to touch him. He was almost a foot taller than she was, big although not built up, and had a bit of a pot belly. In her mind she ran her hands over his tummy, up the sides of his rib cage, and then over his back just below his shoulders. She could almost feel her breasts pressing against the lower part of his chest. And his arms around her. Candy was getting into the action now. Especially when she thought about his hard cock pushing against her belly. Oh yes, Candy was so hungry to feel that warm hardness burrowing sweetly into her folds. She was crying for it. Hot slick tears. Ella moistened the tips of her fingers in Candy's tears and teased the hard button of her clit. Oh yes.

Roger was fucking her now. She could feel his weight. Her hands were caressing his sides and back. He was grunting with pleasure. He was telling her how much he loved fucking her. He was cumming. He was cumming. And so was she.

Ella swam back into an awareness of the sunny Sunday morning. There was an edge of disappointment in her pleasure, though. This Roger was a fantasy. The real Roger would never hold her in his arms. After awhile she got up and put on her bathrobe. Maybe she'd turn on her computer and look into that GFF personals site a friend had told her about.

ROGER SAW ELLA WALK down the sidewalk of the apartment building next door with her two dogs on their leashes. It seemed like an excellent time to take a walk himself. His daughter was in school so he was alone. He timed it so that they'd meet at the end of the sidewalk to his building.

"Hi Ella," he said. "I was headed down to the 7-11."

"These mutts were bugging me to take them out in the worst way. I'm trying to figure out if they own me or I own them."

"I know what you mean," Roger said. "My first wife's toy poodle had her wrapped around his little paw."

"You're on your second wife?"

Roger took a deep breath. Ella could see the look of pain in his face and it made her heart go out to him.

"I'm on no wife. My second divorced me too. And I couldn't even tell you why."

"I've been divorced twice too," Ella said. "I know how much it hurts."

Roger nodded. "Well, I'd better get to the store before Amy gets home."

"Okay. Nice to chat with you."

"Same here."

She's divorced. Roger thought to himself as he walked down the street. Maybe there's hope after all. He got so carried away in thinking about Ella that he walked right past the 7-11 and had to back track. He was still deep in thought when he got home. A plan was taking shape in his mind. Now, if he could find the courage to implement it.

That night, after making sure Amy was tucked in, he lay in his bed. He felt restless. He'd kept his bathrobe on in case he decided to go out into the living room and watch TV. But the thought wasn't very appealing at the moment. He wondered what Ella was doing right now. He fumbled his hand between the folds of the robe and found his cock. It was half hard. It felt good to hold it in his hand. He imagined Ella, naked, on all fours on the edge of his bed, her legs spread apart. He could feel the smooth skin of her bottom under his hand. He was hard now. His fingers were finding the juicy opening of her cunt. Probing into her. She was wet. She was moaning. He knew she wanted him. Wanted him to fuck her. Fuck her deep. He was watching his cock slide between the full cheeks of her ass. And she was pushing against him. She was saying, "Fuck me Roger, Oh Roger, fuck me." And he was shooting his cum out over his chest and belly.

ELLA HAD BEEN ON the GFF site for a week now. She'd spent a lot of time on it and was getting the hang of things. At the moment she was updating her profile, adding more information. She'd had some responses to the first profile she'd put on but, although a couple looked promising, most of them didn't appeal to her at all. They were either too short, too crude, or contained a penis pic without a face. As if any of that was going to make fall on her back and spread her legs.

She'd also browsed through the listings of men in Mississippi and Tennessee. Again, some sounded promising but most of them seemed too single minded. Simple minded. But there was one she liked a lot. And he lived nearby, his profile said. He hadn't included a photo but she felt that his words came from the heart. He said he wanted sex but in an open human way. Reading between the lines she could feel his loneliness. It made her hurt for him.

She'd found herself going back and reading his profile again and again. Once she'd finished her new profile and clicked to update it she went to read his profile once more. And, on impulse, sent him a "wink".

ROGER LOGGED ON TO GFF. But he was beginning to wonder why he bothered. He still had his long distance friends but it seemed that finding someone close by was a lost cause. His home page came up and he saw that he'd received a "wink" from a woman whose handle was "Friend4u". He opened her profile. And liked what he saw. But when he thought about contacting her a heavy weariness fell over him. He wasn't up to dealing with another disappointment. He logged out and shut down his computer.

On his way to the kitchen he glanced out the window and saw Ella walking her dogs towards her apartment. It was time to put his plan in motion.

"Amy," he called. "How'd you like to go out to eat?"

His daughter ran into the room with her face aglow. "Awesome, Dad."

"Do you mind if I invite a friend to come along?"

Amy's face closed down a little but Roger didn't notice. "No, that's okay, Dad."

They walked across to Ella's apartment building. He knocked on the door he'd seen her enter once while driving by. Her front door was on the opposite side of the building from his apartment.

ELLA HAD BEEN WATCHING from her window. The moment she'd realized that he and Amy were headed in her direction she knew what was going to happen. It made her sick with anxiety. She prayed she was wrong. Her husband looked at her from his easy chair when the knock came, glancing away from the TV. She walked to the door, her heart twisting in her chest.

"Come in Roger," she said, trying to sound cheerful. "I'd like you to meet my husband and my daughter."

She could see that the news that she was married appalled him. His face went white. It made her almost want to cry.

"Uhh, no, I'm sorry," he mumbled. "I thought. You said you were divorced and I thought. God, I'm sorry. I was going to ask you out for a hamburger. Never mind." He turned and left abruptly, holding Amy's hand. Now she was crying, turning her head as she passed her husband's chair. He didn't seem to see her tears.

ROGER FELT DEVASTATED. And like a fool. He should have made sure Ella was available before blundering in the way he had. Why did it have to be so hard to find a woman willing to hold him in her arms? And not simply a warm body, but a friend as well? Why did this have to hurt so goddamned much?

Amy seemed to sense his upset and made little girl gestures to try to comfort him. It made him feel even worse to think that she felt the need to do this. He felt like a failure.

Their dining out experience wasn't a very happy one. Nothing like he'd imagined. Now the thoughts of Ella were like arrows being shot through his body.

IT HAD BEEN TWO WEEKS since Roger's visit. They'd avoided each other. The one time they'd slipped up they only exchanged tense smiles. Ella felt so bad. She should have been more careful and made sure he understood that she was married. At odd moments the memory of the look on his face when he grasped the situation stabbed into her heart. She hated knowing she'd hurt someone like that. All because of a misunderstanding that could have been avoided.

Her husband and daughter had gone out for the day, a rare occurrence, and for the first time in a while she was in the mood to play again. She logged on to GFF and checked her email. Nothing much there. For a change she did take a look at a couple of the penis pics. Wondering if she would ever again feel one of those darling man parts moving inside her. She felt like screaming. She was famished for some kind of real interaction.

She'd never tried the GFF Instant Messenger. She'd tried the chatrooms and discovered she didn't like them; too difficult to figure out who wanted the same thing, not to mention hectic and confusing. But maybe the Instant Messenger would work better. She found that there was a list of those currently using the system and began to go through them, selecting the handles that sounded interesting and looking up their profiles.

ROGER HAD ALSO LOGGED ON to the GFF Instant Messenger. He hadn't been able to connect with any of his long distance friends for two days now. There had been a woman he'd enjoyed exchanging emails with who said she only used the GFF Instant Messenger for chatting. He started searching through the listings of those online, hoping to find her. After fifteen minutes of scrolling through the list of handles he was ready to give up. It was then he noticed that "Friend4u" was there.

He sat back in his chair and looked at his monitor. Was it worth it to send her a message? She'd probably ignore him. But God, he felt so lonely. What the fuck?

ELLA WAS GETTING TIRED of going through profiles. Nobody was grabbing her attention. She'd put her hand on the mouse to click out of the system when a message from "Needafriend" popped up on her screen. Oh shit. This was the guy she'd liked so much. It took her a minute to gather herself.

"Hi Needafriend, good to hear from you," she wrote. "I sent you a wink once."

"I got it," Needafriend replied. "Unfortunately I wasn't in a very good place at the time. A lot of things weren't working out."

"I understand how that goes. Hope things are better."

"Not really. But thanks for caring."

The conversation went on. And the longer it did the more excited Ella became. He seemed like a nice guy. He told it like it was without trying to play games. And then he mentioned that he had a webcam.

"I've enjoyed doing that," Friend4u wrote. "I've watched a couple of guys."

"Well, we can't do it through this system. Do you have Yahoo Instant Messenger?"

"Yes, I do. The handle is the same."

"Ok, hang on, I'll contact you."

Within minutes she was watching him. He was naked. She liked his body, big with the beginnings of a pot belly, and a nice cock. Very hard. She could imagine taking him in her mouth.

"Could I see your face?" She typed.

There was a moment of hesitation and then the camera shifted upwards. She almost passed out. It was Roger.

IT TOOK ROGER A MOMENT to decide whether or not to show his face. This was a small town and he had no idea who "Friend4u" was. But, since she was also on GFF, she must be looking for much the same thing as he was so he took the chance. It seemed to take forever for "Friend4u" to respond.

"You there?" He typed.

"I'm here," she replied. "I think I've seen you somewhere."

"That's possible," he typed.

"Show me your cock again."

AS THE CAMERA SLANTED down again Ella felt herself. Oh yes, Candy was weeping again. But these were tears of joy. She opened her legs wide, treasuring her arousal. Now, what was the best way to do this?

"Do you have any special fantasies?" She typed.

"I'm not much for fantasies," Needafriend typed back.

"Is there a woman you know who you think about?"

A moment of hesitation followed. "Yes, there is."

"Tell me about her."

"She lives it the apartment building next door. She's married."

"You like her?"

"God yes. I think she's beautiful. And she seems down to earth. Why are you asking me these questions about another woman?"

"I'm kinky that way. Do you want to fuck her?"

"More than anything in the world."

"Are you alone?"

"Yes. Why do you ask? This conversation is getting strange."

Ella didn't bother to answer. She was tearing off her bathrobe. She headed for the bedroom. It took only a moment to slip into a dress. She didn't bother to put anything on underneath. Moments later she was standing at his door.

"It was me, Roger," she said when he opened the door. He was standing behind it with his head sticking out.

"What do you mean?" He asked.

"I'm the one who just asked if you were alone."

He goggled at her. That's the only word she could think of that described his expression. It made up for the pain she'd seen when she'd revealed that she was married.

"I want to fuck you too," she said. "In the worst way. No, I mean in the best possible way."

He opened the door wider and she pushed in. Glancing to the side she could see that he was naked, as he'd been on the webcam. But now he was soft. She headed in the direction she thought would lead to the bedroom. The instant she saw his bed she began pulling the dress over her head.

ROGER FOLLOWED ELLA down the hall in shocked disbelief. His mind was trying to gather in the pieces of reality that had been blown to smithereens. His heart almost stopped at the sudden appearance of her full bottom. And then the rest of her.

"I want you Roger," she said, turning to face him, her large breasts swinging. "I've wanted you for months, Babe. My husband doesn't give me sex and he's given me permission to find a lover. I want you."

The sweet softness of her skin against his was like thirst quenching water in a place of burning sands. He groaned. He was holding her tight, seeking her lips. Her moans of response made him hard. Somehow, neither of them quite remembering, they ended up on the bed with him between her wide spread legs. He was entering her. They moaned in unison at the intensity of their joining. They were both so aroused that they both climaxed within a minute, almost together. He cradled her, kissing her face, still trying to grasp what had just happened. She smiled up at him, running her fingers through his hair. "I take it that's a yes, you do want to be my lover?" She said.

He felt himself getting hard again.

The Blues Man

> Your man's out prowlin' Baby
> Thinks he likes his women tall and thin
> Keep your back door open
> Cause Baby I'll be comin' in

Laura sat in the back of the small club listening to these words filtered through a voice that sounded like gravel being poured down a steel chute. He was a big man and the guitar in his hands almost looked like a toy but the sounds that poured from the speakers were anything but childlike. They were raw and rich and spoke of a world of experience she couldn't even begin to imagine. She looked around the club and saw a few other white faces but most of the listeners were black.

She didn't hang out in blues clubs but she'd turned twenty-one yesterday and had been seeking a place to celebrate her coming of age. The notice in the paper had caught her eye: "J.B. 'The Blues Man' Thompson, two nights only!" It was a name that brought back memories. Her dad loved J.B.'s music and, when in a blues mood, would play his records over and over. So here she was.

> No you don't have to call me
> I know your man is gone again
> Keep your back door open
> And Baby I'll be comin' in

She figured she must have heard "Keep Your Back Door Open" several thousand times. And once, a couple of years ago, her dad, his tongue loosened by wine, had explained to her that the song was referring to anal sex. It kind of grossed her out to have her dad bring up the subject. But now, hearing J.B.'s powerful delivery over the driving rhythm of bass and drums, punctuated by his forceful guitar work, the obvious depth of his experience made her curious. She shifted in her chair.

She didn't have a boyfriend. And would just as soon not think about all that. It was her weight, she felt sure; men didn't see her. Not sexually anyway. She was a pretty face, a buddy, or a sister. Shit. She was here to have a good time, not cry over all the milk that had been spilled in her life. She sipped her screwdriver, the only drink that came to her mind to order when the waitress asked, and decided that once she'd finished this one she would go home.

The set ended and J.B. moved through the audience shaking hands and saying hello. He passed her table and he gave her a look of appreciation before going up to the bar. Several women, much thinner than she, flitted at his elbow. She emptied her glass and was preparing to rise when he turned, ignoring the women around him, and looked at her again. The waitress came and she ordered another screwdriver.

"Are you enjoying the show?" He asked. His speaking voice sounded as if it had been aged in a charred oak barrel. Up close she could see that the years had poured more salt than pepper into his hair.

"Oh yes, Mr. Thompson. I think it's great."

"Jesus. My name's J.B.," he said, "call me J.B. Do you mind if I sit down?"

"Please do. My name's Laura. Laura Hamilton."

He sat and they chatted for a bit. He asked her about herself and seemed genuinely interested in her life. And wished her happy birthday when she mentioned why she was out on the town. He asked about boyfriends and picked up on the feelings of hurt behind her mumbled response. It was a little scary for her to be read so easily by a man she'd only met a few minutes ago. He was calm and a gentleman but there was something in his eyes that told her he didn't think she was just a pretty face, or a buddy. Most certainly, she was not his sister. The drummer and bass player were back on stage and had started to jam. He excused himself, began to walk toward the stage, and then turned and looked at her. Something in his glance made her realize that he was hoping she would stay. When the waitress came she ordered another screwdriver.

As he launched into his next set she realized she was looking at him with new eyes. She had the feeling, somewhere deep inside her, that this man could become her next lover. She knew it was her choice. And as she watched his powerful fingers roaming with delicate precision over the fretboard of his guitar, the one she'd heard he called "Doreen", she could feel her body saying yes. Oh yes. Oh God yes.

"Are you okay?" She jerked up, comprehending with difficulty that he was speaking to her.

"I think I dranktoomush," she said, knowing she was slurring her words together. From a distance, filled with cotton balls and blurred images, she heard his full, but not unfriendly, laughter. The room was empty except for several people cleaning up.

"Have you got a way home, girl," he said.

"I druvv. I wanna go home wichew," she tried to enunciate. More laughter.

"I don't have a home here. But I've got a motel room with a bed big enough for two."

"Thashsoundswonderfl," was her response.

She never could remember getting from the club to a taxicab. She did have a dim memory of him telling the cabbie to stop and then opening the door. She'd leaned out and thrown up into the street. She sort of recalled his strong fingers holding her and his voice. His warm rough voice telling her it was all right. It was cool.

The next thing she remembered was waking up. She was lying on her side. The wall of a room she'd never seen before in her life was staring her in the face. Someone, and at the moment she couldn't recollect who, was making soft snoring sighs behind her. Oh shit. She surreptitiously felt herself. She was naked. Oh shit. Damn. Her head ached and she tried to recollect what might have happened. All she could find was blankness. Oh Jesus Lord. What had awakened her was a bladder that insisted on being emptied. She wished she could shrivel up and disappear. How did she get into this?

She drew the sheet and blanket back and slid her legs out till her feet touched the floor. She pulled herself up, leaned over, her breasts squashed against her knees, and gazed at the floor. Her head was swirling; her stomach was very unhappy with her. Oh shit. The maid had missed a few spots when she vacuumed. Little bits of grit. I think I'm in Hell, she thought. Without warning a large hand was on her back, just above her ass. She jumped.

"Are you okay?" A huge voice rumbled.

"Hmmyeahi'mfine," she said. She turned and found herself gazing into a face she'd seen so often on LP album covers. "Oh shit. Oh God in heaven." The memories of the previous evening came stampeding back into her consciousness.

"You're okay. It's cool, baby." The warm, rough, and familiar voice said. "I didn't take advantage of a poor white girl in distress."

"I'm naked. Where are my clothes?"

"You puked on your dress, honey," the voice from her dad's record library said. "I didn't think you'd want to sleep in it. And once I got your dress off I figured what the hell."

She looked into his eyes. He looked straight back at her. She felt calm.

"Thank you," she said.

"Girl, you're more than welcome. Now take that piss. I know you need to."

She laughed as she sat on the toilet and let go. She laughed knowing he could hear her laugh and the flow of her urine. She laughed knowing he accepted all this human stuff and still wanted to fuck her. She laughed because something inside herself felt free.

"Well, look at what the pussy dragged home," she said, posing in front of the bathroom door. Her head throbbed and her tummy was mumbling cuss words.

"Hmmmm. Pussy's an excellent judge of what I like," he said. "But let's get some breakfast first. It's only eleven o'clock in the morning and no one's expecting me to be anywhere until eight in the evening or so."

She was amazed at how free she felt being naked around him. And it touched her deeply to realize that he'd, with great care, washed the vomit out of her dress and hung it over the curtain rod. Something she'd hadn't noticed while she was peeing. Which wasn't surprising, considering the state she'd been in.

They interacted as if they were they'd been married for many years. She peeked in while he was shaving and enjoyed the sight of his bulky blackness in front of the mirror. He, fully dressed, and talking with one of his music business contacts on the phone, watched her slip into her lingerie and wrinkled dress.

"Well, I do all right," he said, in response to the question she'd posed at the the breakfast table. "I make a living. I'm no B.B. King but I do all right." Then, with clear seriousness, he said, "I love what I do." He held up his fingers and moved them as if playing a guitar. "And I love to fuck. It works out. I wouldn't trade it for anything."

Later, back in the motel room, after the food and a nap had cleared away most of her hangover, she felt those fingers playing her as if she were some fine instrument. As if she were Doreen. He traveled effortlessly up the octaves until she was crying out for him to stop. And then it was his cock. She was gazing up into his eyes, eyes it seemed she'd always known, feeling him move inside her. She opened her legs as wide as they'd go. He held himself above her, careful not to overwhelm her with his weight, and slowly slid back and forth. His motions were easy and deliberate and it was obvious to her that he was feeling a great deal of pleasure. She put her hand on his thick arm and marveled at her whiteness against his blackness. He smiled down at her.

"Does it feel good, Baby?" He asked.

"Oh, God yes, J.B." They both looked down to watch his black length sliding between the lips of her sparsely haired pussy. "You're the first black man I've ever been with."

"I'm a man like any other, not all that much difference."

"We're different colors," she said. "I like seeing the contrast."

"Oh, yeah, there's that. I like it too. I like your body," he said, supporting himself on one hand and reaching out to touch her left breast with the other.

"I'm too fat," she said, her soul shrinking.

"I like your body, as I said," he stated with a bit of an edge. "You've got a beautiful body and some of the sweetest skin I've ever touched."

She wasn't convinced but felt herself relax, though not completely. And then he was moving in her powerfully, the earlier finesse transformed into an exuberant all out physical engagement. His big hands clasped her ass cheeks. His cock plunged into her. He moaned into her neck, reporting his progress towards orgasm. It excited her. She felt herself pulled along. She felt pleased to be able to give him this. And then they were there. She could feel him coming inside her. And moments later she was crying out to him that her own climax was crashing through her.

He held her, making gentle comforting sounds. Almost as if she were a fearful child. He held her for a long time. Longer than any other man she'd been with. When he pulled away she could see a big smile on his face.

"Oh, that was good, baby. Thank you."

"Thank *you*, J.B.," she said. She touched herself and felt the thick slickness of his semen. Then she reached out and grasped his cock which showed only slight signs of hardness. "Are we going to be able to do this again?"

He laughed. "Yeah, Baby," he said. "Give me a little time. I'm not as young as I used to be."

A little over an hour later, after she'd treated him to the loving attention of her mouth and tongue, he was hard once more.

"My back door's open too, J.B.," she said.

He looked at her with his large heavy lidded eyes. "You know what that song's a talkin' about?"

She rolled over on her tummy and wiggled her butt.

He threw his head back and laughed his deep smoky laugh. "Yes, I guess you do." He sat up and opened the drawer next to the bed and pulled out a small bottle of lube.

"Goodness, you came prepared," she said.

"I have a certain reputation to maintain," he growled, and then laughed.

"I want you to do me in my behind but I've never done it before," she said anxiously.

He looked at her. "You want me to be your first?"

She nodded.

He spread her cheeks and stared as if he wanted to see inside her. Then she felt his big tongue tickling her anus. "You've got to relax, girl," he said after a few minutes. "This is not going to feel good unless you relax." Several minutes later he poured lube on her and began opening her up with his finger. She felt how gentle and careful he was and her sphincter muscles began to loosen. "Oh yeah, baby, that's it," he said.

"What would your Daddy think a you havin' a black man's cock in your ass?" He asked, slowly entering her.

"He's got all your records," was her reply. "He was the one who told me 'Keep Your Back Door Open' was about anal sex."

J.B. roared. The bed shook with the force of his laughter. Tears ran down his face. "Oh Jesus. Oh Jesus. Well, he sure raised a sweet girl child."

"Is this the kind of thing a sweet girl child would do? A sweet fat girl child, at that?" She asked, moving her butt against him, a little surprised by the bitterness in her voice.

An instant later he was dead serious. "Girl, this is as sweet as it gets. Don't put yourself down. You're a beautiful woman, a loving woman. Don't be afraid to shake your ass at the world and make it pay attention. Nobody be thinking you're somethin' till you think you're somethin' yourself."

Several moments later he said, "I'm old enough to be your granddaddy so I know a thing or two." They both laughed at the incongruity of an older man saying this to a young woman he was fucking in the ass.

"Ok Granddad," she said. "I'll remember that."

"You better," he said, giving her a couple of good hard strokes. "Will this help your memory?"

"Oh yeah. Oh yeah." She cried. A kind of orgasm she'd never

experienced before flowed through her. Volcanic heat centered around her rectum, flowing like lava through her bowels. "Oh shit. Oh shit."

"You're gonna make me cum, baby, you keep yellin' like that," he called in his powerful voice.

"Oh yeah, cum in my ass J. B. Fill me with your hot cum," she moaned. She felt him clench her ass cheeks in his two strong hands and then bury himself.

"Here it comes, baby. Oh Jesus. Oh Jesus."

And then, deep within her body, she felt his pulsing. Dim sparks of warmth. But what she felt most were his arms clenching themselves around her, moments later, tight against her breasts, holding her as they both rode the waves of pleasure. And his big belly against her back. He held her, as he had before; it made her realize that when she found her life partner she wanted him to do this.

They rode together to the club where she picked up her car, drove home to take a shower and change her dress, and then drove back to the club. This time she drank soda. When he finished his last set she took him back to the motel and they made love again.

They said goodbye over breakfast and hugged before she climbed into her car.

"Now remember, nobody be thinking you're somethin' till you think you're somethin' yourself," were his final words. She repeated them to herself often.

She began to follow his touring through his site on the Internet and the next time he was in town she took her dad and her new boyfriend, Earl, to see him. He recognized her immediately and between sets came over to sit with them. Earl and her dad were astounded. She told them that the last time J.B. had played here she'd spent a little time with him. Neither man cared to inquire further. She could see that her dad was awestruck to be in the presence of a man he'd admired for so many years and, consequently, a little in awe of his daughter who could hobnob with his idol with such ease. Before they left J.B. caught her coming out of the women's restroom.

"You look happy," he said.

"I am," she smiled.

"Well, you deserve to be. Keep workin' it." He kissed her chastely on the cheek. And then, much less chastely, squeezed her ass.

She walked out into the club to find Earl and her dad. A warm giggle bubbled inside her.

Ocean Interlude

It had been a long day but finally, after six hours of riding an old rickety bus filled with locals down the twisting mountain roads, they had come to the sea. To Alicia it was like entering the open arms of a large-breasted, warm-hearted, mother who welcomed her home.

She was traveling light. Her new backpack was giving her trouble and she missed the old one, the smaller one she'd given her kid brother. This one made her feel awkward, off balance. It caught on the door as she stepped off the bus and almost caused her to bang her head. She cursed softly, under her breath.

She was sweaty and dirty. She could smell herself as well as the others around her. Standing on the road, half numb with fatigue, she tried to decide between the sterile comfort of a rented bungalow or pitching the tent on the beach beside the thundering ocean. Her legs moved almost without her volition; she needed the sea. She'd been away too long.

As she followed the path to the beach she looked at the watch she kept in her pocket and discovered that it was four in the afternoon. Still plenty of time to set up camp. Now out of the trees she walked onto the soft sand and looked out over the immense vista of moving water. Her fatigue lifted as she took a deep breath of the pungent air and listened to the crash of the surf. With lighter steps she began heading down the beach in search of a secluded spot.

The rest of the afternoon and early evening was spent putting up her tent, arranging her bedclothes and cooking gear, gathering firewood, and taking a much needed nap. When she awoke the sun was plunging into the ocean in a blaze of red that painted both the water and the sky. Emerging from the tent she stretched and looked around. There was no one to be seen. Alicia unbuttoned her shirt, pulled it away from her full bare breasts, and threw it inside the tent. A moment later her jeans and underwear followed. After unbinding her long black hair she bent down, picked up her small bar of soap and towel, and walked to the shore.

Dropping the towel in dry sand she strode into the water. It exhilarated her to feel the soft air and cool water on her naked skin, the current pushing against her breasts when the waves surged in. Salt water, she knew, wasn't the best to use for cleaning but she decided she'd at least be cleaner than she'd been. Rubbing the bar of soap under her armpits, down her arms, across her breasts and belly, between her legs, and, finally, between the cheeks of her bottom, she felt lighter as the dusty grit was washed away.

Collecting her towel, and shaking out the sand, she dried herself off. Once more looking up and down the beach. Again there was no one in sight. She walked back to the tent enjoying her nakedness, hung the towel on the tent rope, and rubbed mosquito repellant over her body. Squatting down she began to assemble her fire.

After eating she lay back on a blanket and watched the dying embers. Then looked up to take in the brilliant parade of sparkling stars as the waves crashed against the sand. This was so different from the day to day stress of running a business. Without giving it much thought she began to touch her body. Alicia could feel herself start to get excited. It felt so good. She opened her legs wide, giving the stars an intimate view of her soft inner lips. She tested the mouth of her vagina with her fingers and found the first traces of dampness. Her other hand began to play with her breasts and she gently teased her clitoris, feeling it swell. Testing her vagina again she found a slickness that she transferred to her clit. She could feel her excitement burgeoning.

As her fingers danced on her body she looked into the heavens. She had a sense of opening herself to the cosmos. Of being fucked by the sound of the ocean. Of being made love to by the silky breeze and the thick scents of the earth. Of being seen by the stars as she shuddered with orgasm. And minutes later shuddered again. And once more. Sated she climbed into her tent and fell into a deep happy sleep.

Next day she was awakened at dawn by the calls of birds, and the annoying "knock- knock" of a woodpecker that had decided to make his home next to hers. She popped her head out of the tent and looked right and left. There was nobody but a solitary man on a horse coming slowly, still far away. Naked, she sprinted and dived into the sea.

She swam vigorously for ten minutes and stopped to rest on her back. The man on the horse was getting close now. Alicia stood up to take a better look. It was an old man, with white hair and a long white beard. He looked tired and sad. The horse was a dark dirty grey and seemed as sad as his owner.

On a whim Alicia jumped out of the water a couple of times, as high as she was able to. Waving to the old man. He stared hard, trying to make sense of the apparition. A naked woman, with generous breasts bouncing wildly, rich brown skin, and untamed long black hair seemed to want his attention.

The merest hint of a smile appeared in the old man's eyes, he waved back at the sea angel and continued his solitary journey.

Alicia swam for another ten minutes and got out of the water. She was starving. After having a cup of tea and some cheese and crackers, she put on a pair of shorts, a long t-shirt, and grabbed her sandals. She'd decided to do a little exploring.

She hadn't been to this part of the coast in 5 or 6 years, but she had a vague memory of a small river a kilometer or so south from where she had pitched her tent. She wondered about taking her bathing suit but decided not to.

She walked along the beach looking at the crabs running away from the foaming water. She took a deep breath and thought that the decision of dropping everything and escaping from the office for a week had been the best thing to do. The deal was off, but it had not been her fault. Far from it. But she still felt annoyed at herself thinking that if she had tried this or that, maybe Mark wouldn't have made a fool of himself. It was too late now. In a week or so she would go back to the city, pick up the pieces, and start again. This time Mark would have to go; she had given him a chance and he'd blown it. It made her head ache to think about the whole mess.

Lost in her somber thoughts it took her a moment to realize she'd found the little river. Well, it was more as if she'd stumbled on it. She stepped over a piece of dead wood on the bank and had a good look around. It wasn't a river, she realized, more like a creek. The waters were clear because it hadn't rained in a couple of days. Otherwise the water would be brown, full of leaves and dead branches.

It was getting hot now, not a single cloud on sight. The sky was deep blue, so bright it hurt to look at it. She blinked several times and managed to get a few tears to soothe the smarting.

Funny, she thought, the creek didn't look like the one she

remembered. But then, the shore line changed continuously on this side of the coast. The tides shaped the sands everyday, like a hand playing carelessly with clay. One day there were trees near the beach and a couple of days later some of them had disappeared. So too was the course of the creek changed by the sand that kept invading it.

She followed the creek inland for a while, trying to get close to a noise she heard. The distance was deceptive, she walked for at least ten minutes before she found a water fall. It was about two meters high, but the rocks and the vegetation surrounding it made it echo strangely. She got into the water and splashed her face and arms, looking at the blue and orange butterflies skimming the surface of the water.

Yielding to temptation she took off her few clothes and went and stood right below the waterfall. The water was massaging her back and she turned round to feel it on her breasts. She turned round again, closed her eyes, and imagined that she was being cleansed of all worries and aches.

She began to caress her breasts gently. Her right hand went down to her pubic hair, playing with it. She rubbed her clitoris ever so gently. She sighed softly, opened her legs wider and inserted one finger in her warm vagina, her other hand playing with her left breast.

Something made her open her eyes. In front of her a boy, of at least eighteen years, was staring at her incredulously, his face turning a dusky shade of red. He had a small net on one arm and the other hand had probably held the now emptying bucket of river shrimps. He wore no shirt, a pair of very short old trunks and an erection.

He and Alicia stared at one another in stunned silence for several long moments. She still had her finger inside herself. Then the boy looked down at the fallen bucket. He took a deep breath and looked up again. She could see the desire in his eyes. And the uncertainty. She ran her eyes over his body and liked what she saw, half boy softness and half adult strength. She withdrew her finger and stepped out of the falling water. He took a short step back, his eyes on her forest of pubic hair. The intensity of his gaze, as it rose up her body, excited her. When his eyes reached her face she smiled encouragingly.

Alicia reached out her hand. After long seconds of hesitation he threw the net on to the bank and walked to her, taking her hand. She slid her right hand around his smooth young body and pulled him close as their lips met. His hardness pressed against her belly.

At first his kiss was tentative but as he felt her tongue reaching out, seeking his, he responded avidly. His mouth tasted sweet and good to her. They were both grunting quietly, sighing with pleasure. With her full breasts squashed against his broad chest they kissed with growing passion.

Her fingers found the waistband of his trunks and pushed them down over his firm buttocks. The heat of his cock now burned against her skin. He groaned into her mouth as she wrapped her hand around him. She could feel the trembling warmth of arousal in her belly as she held his rigid cock. Even as she'd fingered herself under the water the creamy dew had begun coating her inner walls but now she knew she must be drenched. Her cunt began to ache to be entered.

He, knowing she was available to him, grew impatient, almost brutal. He was like a young animal lost in rut. She gave herself over and let him half drag her to a patch of shaded grass. Then he was pushing her down, spreading her legs. With a loud groan he entered her. The feeling of surrender and the sensations of his cock moving inside her were very exciting. She rubbed both hands over the smooth skin of his back and buttocks as he bucked on top of her. All too quickly she felt the pulsing of his climax. And his body fell on hers like a heavy rain, in his own surrender.

"Ah, mi amor (Ah, my love)," she sighed, caressing him. "Mi dulce amante (my sweet lover)."

Lying together, her arms around him, they talked quietly. She told him that she was camping on the beach and he asked if he could visit her. She laughed softly and kissed him. Saying she'd like that very much. Almost at once he became hard and she laughed again.

"Ah mi amor, que voy a hacer contigo? (what am I going to do with you?)" She said.

"Puedo pensar en algunas cosas (I can think of some things)," he said, growing bolder now he felt himself to be a man.

"Necesitas pescar mas camarones para tu familia (You need to catch more shrimp for your family)," she said. "Si puedes ven a mi esta noche (Come to me tonight, if you can)."

They dressed and parted after embracing and kissing several times. She felt herself glowing and began to hum an old folk song. It was the middle of the afternoon when she got back to her tent. She found a spot in the shade for her siesta. She had a feeling she would need her rest. When she awoke, the old man from that morning was squatting beside his horse with a bouquet of wild flowers in his hand.

"Toma esto (Take these)," he said. "Le diste a un viejo un dia de felicidad, mi bella mujer de la mar (You gave an old man a day of happiness, my beautiful woman of the sea).

She took the flowers and kissed his hairy cheek. He grinned hugely, showing his broken teeth, and climbed, with some difficulty, back onto his horse. "Tal vez manana temprano abuelo (Perhaps again tomorrow morning, grandfather)," she said.

"Entonces tendré dos dias de felicidad (Then I will have two days of happiness)," he said, and rode slowly away.

She put the flowers in a small pot and then made a fire and fixed herself something to eat. It was close to sundown, sometime after she'd eaten and washed her dishes, when she saw the boy walking up the beach towards her. He wore a clean shirt and shorts and carried a small bottle of wine. She rose to her feet and greeted him, but her kisses weren't as passionate as they'd been earlier in the day. She could feel his eagerness and sensed his disappointment when she restrained him.

"Ten calma querido, tenemos tiempo (Take it easy dear, there is time)" she said softly.

They sat and talked for awhile, drinking the wine from her one enameled cup. She made sure that neither of them drank too much. She took his hand and put it on her breast. He didn't have any difficulty deciphering her invitation. His mouth found hers and their clothes seemed to melt away. Once more it was hard and quick and once more she didn't come.

She began to talk to him of love, and sex, and women. She fondled his balls and stroked his half hard cock and talked about her pleasure, her needs. She told him about her secret places. About the place along her rib cage, just below her breasts, where she loved to feel a man touch her as he moved inside her. About the place on top of her head where a man's fingers rubbing her as she came would make her orgasm so much more intense. For a time she was silent as she took his cock in her mouth, marveling at the smoothness of it against her tongue, and then, when it was hard, climbed astride him and took him inside. She rode him, controlling his movements, and talked.

She told him that every woman's body was a little different. That each woman had her own secret places. She sought to communicate to him the rewards that would be his if he cared enough to ask a woman to show him where her secret places were. She revealed to him that many women didn't even know about their secret places. She told him that he and his lover would have to explore together and find them.

She explained to him that some women liked sweet talk at all times. Some women liked dirty talk. Some women liked sweet talk at first and then dirty talk as they approached orgasm. And some liked different talk at different times. He would have to ask questions and listen carefully to the answers. Patience, empathy, and laughter, she revealed, were the keys to a woman's heart.

And she soon learned that he was listening. As she moved above him he reached up and stroked the sides of her rib cage. And then, as she sensed the waves of her climax rising within, and told him so, she felt his fingers at the top of her head. The stars smiled when they heard her cries of joy.

For the next six days they were often together. She taught him about a woman's body. She opened herself and showed him. She shared with him the ways to use his mouth and tongue to give her the deepest pleasure. To her delight she found he was an apt pupil. And one who understood the need for practice.

She never saw the old man again. She and the boy slept late. But one morning when they crawled out of the tent she discovered a bouquet of wild flowers. The boy was curious and she told him the story. It warmed her heart to see him smile gently as he thought of the old man watching her. This boy was going to be a beautiful man, she was sure.

"Ah, mi amor," she said on the last day. "Debo marcharme (I must leave)." They were both very sad. They lay and held each other for a long long time. At last she pulled away and packed her belongings. After one last kiss she left him sitting on the beach.

She climbed aboard the dilapidated bus and found a seat. She thought of her young lover and smiled. She knew she'd left behind her a boy who'd become a man who would know how to give his women pleasure. Who would know the signs. And who would care enough to make sure his lover was satisfied. The bus began the slow trek over the mountains and her mind moved forward, thinking about how she was going to handle the situation with Mark. And how she was going to find his replacement. She realized, with calm contentment, that the time by the ocean had changed her attitude.

Her spirit was full and clear again. She was ready for whatever the world might choose to throw at her.

Win/Win Situation

Over two months had passed since Jake Barlow escaped from the prison in Tennessee. The first two or three weeks had been rough. First, on foot, he'd headed for Gainesville, Georgia, because that's where a buddy of his had been living the last he'd known. When he got there, however, he learned that his friend was long gone. The local news reports, because he'd spent some time in the area, made frequent references to his escape. And his old acquaintances couldn't show him the door fast enough. He was glad that none of them had turned him in.

The whole thing pissed him off. Sure he was guilty. He wasn't the kind of guy to whine about how innocent he was. But it was only a couple of minor burglaries. The judge, a doddering old motherfucker, got a hair up his butt and sentenced him to ten years without the possibility of parole. His lawyer, a young kid from the Public Defender's office, said it wasn't even legal. And then didn't lift a finger to make an appeal. Jake was sure that it was his Indian blood, his being one quarter Cherokee, that got the old judge all stirred up and made the punk kid apathetic. Shit. Double shit, fuck, damn.

Prison had been hell. He loved his freedom. And he didn't tend to like other men. A few buddies, and that was it. But God did he love women and there weren't any at the prison he'd been in. No inmates. Not even female guards. He'd been able to exchange photos of naked women with a couple of guys on the outside but, in a way, it made things worse. He'd look at the photos and it would almost make him want to explode. Imagining their warm soft bodies against his made him want to yell at the top of his lungs and go climbing up the bars of his cell.

He'd made it through four and a half years before he decided he had to get out. It took another eight months before he could work out a plan and make it happen. And now he was out, had been for nine weeks.

For awhile, in the early spring, after hitting the dead ends in Gainesville, he'd hung out around the lakes. Shit, he was a burglar by trade, it wasn't that hard to get his hands on what he needed. Clothes, food, a tent, and an occasional bottle of booze. The one thing he hadn't been able to find was a woman. And he was a passionate man. He loved to fuck. He was used to fucking a lot before going to prison. All that desire had backed up in his system. His balls were so full they ached and felt as heavy as lead weights. He had an almost constant hard on. While in prison he'd thought about finding a pretty boy and fucking some of that desire out but it wasn't the same. He couldn't do it. And no one sure as hell messed with him. He wasn't, by nature, a violent man but he was big and strong. A couple of short encounters with the meanest of the mean alerted everyone in the prison that he could take care of himself.

While living near the lakes, setting his tent up in remote areas, he'd begun using a pair of stolen binoculars to scan the waters for female forms. Often enough, usually on weekends, he'd see a few. He felt as if he was trying to drink them in through the eye pieces of his binoculars. One time he got lucky. He still found it hard to believe.

A man and a woman had dropped anchor in a secluded cove across the lake, about quarter of a mile away. The woman, much to Jake's amazement, had almost immediately taken off her clothes. Every fucking stitch. The guy had done the same but with less enthusiasm. And Jake didn't give a shit about the guy anyway. Oh Jesus, she was cute. Big bobbling boobs and a nice round ass. Delicious jiggles all the way around. He'd thought very seriously of swimming across and laying it to her. But decided against jeopardizing his sanctuary. As it was he memorized every detail of her body.

The couple swam to shore at one point and disappeared into the woods. Jake knew damn well what was going on. That sweet cunt was getting fucked. She had her legs spread open and a cock inside her. Jake hated to jerk off. It seemed like a waste. If he wasn't shooting his seed into or onto a woman's body it was a total loss, as far as he was concerned. But he had to jerk off now. He was taking her from behind, rutting like a dog, watching her big young ass quiver as he pounded into her. He could hear her moaning. She was saying, "Fuck me, God yes, fuck me." He could almost feel it. Almost see it. Almost hear. When he came it was like a freak of nature. Shooting sprays of pearly cum he tossed his head back and screamed like a panther. A male panther calling to his mate. But it left him feeling so empty afterwards. God have mercy, he needed a woman. A real woman. One as hungry to fuck as he was.

That was six weeks ago now and the memory of that cutie's naked body was still enough to almost drive him insane. His balls had that deep heavy ache again. And he couldn't remember losing his erection even once in all that time.

They'd almost caught him down at the lakes. A couple of boaters saw him and his instincts told him to get out. He was already on the move when the chopper started making passes over the place where he'd been. That night he'd stolen an outboard, pushed to the northern edge of the lakes, and then continued north on foot after sinking the boat. In a shed outside a summer cabin he'd found a dirt bike which made traveling a lot easier as long as he was careful not to draw attention to himself.

Now he was holed up not far from Dahlonega, Georgia. It was small enough for the cops to be laid back but big enough to supply the things he needed. And because of the tourist traffic and the University he didn't stand out like a dog at a cat party as he would have in most other small southern towns. Over the weeks he'd been here he'd begun to cautiously explore the area.

DARLENE JEFFERSON HAD THE day off. And she was feeling lazy. There was nothing she had to do so she'd taken her time getting out of bed, showering, and fixing breakfast. Now she was sitting at the table finishing her last cup of coffee and trying to decide what to do with the rest of the day. She had the TV turned on with the sound down low. The flickering images gave a kind of companionship. The news was on, she noticed idly. The photo of a man's face flashed on the screen. Oh yeah, Darlene thought, That Jake Barlow guy.

A couple of her friends had told her they were concerned about her living alone, as isolated as she was. The way the woods came right up to her backyard would make it easy for a man like Jake Barlow to sneak onto the property and do whatever he wanted with her. Yeah, right, she thought. I wish he would. I could use a man. But the last I heard he was down south.

The thought made her squirm a little in her chair. Even that quick passing idea had made her pussy respond. She could feel the familiar ache, the tightening of her clit. Her nipples hurt. This was the longest dry spell in her life and it was making her a little nuts. Sure she had her toys and she made herself cum on a regular basis but it was a poor substitute for having a man hold you in his arms and do what a man does. Especially a man who enjoys a hot woman.

And she was hot. Oh Lord was she. To feel the weight of a man against her skin. His hard cock plunging deep into her pussy. Or, even better, into the depths of her ass. Thinking about it was making her ache painfully. Time to think about something else.

But remembering what her friends had said about her backyard had given her an idea. It was about time she started working on getting some sun. With that in mind she put her breakfast dishes in the dishwasher and went to change into her two piece bathing suit. Within a short time she was lying on her stomach, after applying suntan oil, feeling the hot sun soaking into her skin. She'd unhooked the top of her bathing suit and was lying with her breasts in the cups. After about twenty minutes she decided to turn over. Usually she kept her top on but this morning, for some reason, she decided to leave it off. She rolled over onto her back and then sat up. She spread oil over her body, paying special attention to her breasts. It felt good to massage them. Her nipples hardened. She settled back and considered masturbating. But the sun made her drowsy. She fell asleep.

IT TOOK JAKE BARLOW a second to realize what he was looking at. He'd been reconnoitering the woods since early in the morning. He'd seen the roof of a house from some distance away but had wanted to make sure that there weren't any people around who might catch him by surprise. But, as far as he could tell, he was alone. He'd then begun to approach the house. Because he was thinking like a hunter, watching for movement and listening for tell tale sounds, the figure lying on some kind of mat in the open space between the woods and the house didn't quite register.

And then it slammed into his brain. Pushing the breath from his lungs. He stood there panting like an exhausted cougar. A woman. A half naked woman. He could see the brown circles on her tits even at this distance. His hard on got harder, if that was possible, and started to ache painfully. His balls seemed to swell. He felt his legs shaking.

His body made the decision for him. He wasn't even aware of having had a conscious thought. He was moving towards her pulling off his clothes as he went. The thought crossed his mind that there might be a man in the house who'd come running out with a 357 magnum in his hand to blow this crazy half naked man away. But Jake didn't care at this point. At least he'd die happy. The last few yards he was naked. His cock jutted out from his body and was so hard it barely bobbed as he strode closer. And then he was standing, looking down at her.

And Jesus God in Heaven he liked what he saw. This was a real woman's body, full and soft. Large cushiony tits with brown nipples like big sweet berries. Round ass that could take a pounding. But the part he was most hungry to see was hidden by a piece of cloth. Well, not for long, he thought. He reached down, grasped both sides of the bathing suit bottom, and jerked it down the length of the woman's legs.

DARLENE HAD NO EXPLANATION for what she felt happening. Struggling up into consciousness her first thought was that a huge wind, maybe a tornado, had struck and pulled off her swim suit. It took her a moment to open her eyes. And when she did the reality seemed even stranger. There was a tall muscular naked man standing at her feet with her bathing suit bottoms swinging in his hand. With an impressive hard cock. She glanced at his face and the knowledge of who she was looking at made her gasp.

"Open your legs," he said.

She was numb. She couldn't think. She'd heard what he said and had gotten the gist of what he wanted but her body didn't want to function. What her friends had feared was happening.

"Open your goddamned legs," he said again.

This time the clear anger in his voice cut through her torpor. She hesitantly began to comply.

"Wider. Wide open. I want to see it all."

He scared the hell out of her. Her legs went as wide as they would go. He was looking at her with the intensity of a cutting torch. The same fierce heat. Against her will her body began to respond with a similar hotness.

"Oh God have mercy. Oh sweet Jesus," he said, as he looked at her gaping clean shaven pussy. It was as if he'd seen a man rise from the dead.

There was a powerful note of awe in his voice that made the heat rush through her. No other man had ever looked at her with the same feverous desire she could read in his eyes. She felt a trickle of her juice slide down between the cheeks of her ass. This was something she'd never experienced before. She'd never gotten so turned on so quick.

Without warning he dropped to his knees beside her and thrust two fingers into her cunt hole. It made her groan with pleasure. Her hips bucked up to take his fingers deeper inside.

He looked at her in astonishment. Meeting her eyes. Almost seeing her as a person. "Goddamn, woman, you are so wet. Oh shit I've missed this. Feeling my fingers in a hot woman's cunt. Oh Jesus Lord." He stirred his fingers around inside her. It embarrassed her to hear the wet squishy sounds she made. It was impossible to hide her arousal. And it felt so good. Which made her wetter.

As he finger fucked her with one hand he began running his other hand over her body. He couldn't seem to get enough of the feel of her skin under his fingers. He stroked her belly and sighed. And groaned as he caught the lolling weight of her breasts, plucking and playing with her nipples. With a moan he pressed his chest against her soft stomach and rubbed against her as his long hair fell over her right breast and shoulder. And then he was sucking her left nipple into his mouth.

JAKE FELT INTOXICATED by this woman's full body. By the sweet softness of her skin and the woman scent. And it was clear that she was responding to him. He could sense that she was still frightened but her cunt was crying for his cock.

"Do you want me to fuck you?" Jake asked, lifting his head and looking into her face. "Do you want to feel my hard cock inside you?"

Her nod was almost imperceptible.

"You're going to have to do better than that," he said. "Your cunt is drooling for it." He pulled his fingers out and straddled her torso. Grasping her breasts he pushed their pillowy softness around his big balls and the length of his cock. He grinned to see her eyes fix on the large purple head. "You want to feel that up your cunt? Fucking you? Talk to me."

Her eyes closed. "Yes," she said quietly.

"Louder. I can't hear you."

"Yes," she said.

"Yes, what?"

"Yes, I want you to fuck me."

That was all he needed. Seconds later he was kneeling between her wide open legs. He touched the head of his cock to the mouth of her cunt. "Oh sweet Jesus," he said. He felt the wet warmth close around the first inch. "Oh shit goddamn. God how I've missed this." He was trying to savor every sensation. But the need was too great. He couldn't help it. He had to be as far inside her as he could go. A moment later he was. He gave a deep groaning howl as he felt the warm grip of connection that only being inside a woman could create. "Oh yes. Oh God, yes," he sighed. And then he began fucking her.

DARLENE'S FIRST THOUGHT as Jake began fucking her was, Oh my lord, this man can move. He surged into her with the muscular grace of a large cat. His movements were fluid and powerful and she could feel him touching places inside her that she couldn't remember any other man hitting in quite the same way. She couldn't help but lift herself to meet him as she reached up and stroked his chest and thick arms with her hands. All her fear of him was gone. And as he felt her join him his movements became even more precise and thrilling although she couldn't imagine how that was even possible.

"Oh. Oh," she moaned. "I don't believe this."

Their eyes met and in that instant they were bound together in a tight ring of pleasure.

"You like to fuck, don't you Baby," he said, thrusting into her with long strokes.

"Oh God yes," she moaned, "when it's like this."

He pushed deep inside and began grinding his lower belly against her, engaging her clit. His eyes seemed to glaze over. Then he closed them. Throwing his head back, his face twisted, he grabbed her hips and pounded into her rough and hard. All delicacy forgotten. A second later he made one last hard thrust, went stiff as steel, and screamed like a wild animal. In her depths it felt as if someone had turned on a hose. And then she was coming too.

She assumed that like every other man she'd been with he'd have to stop and recuperate. Or maybe he'd simply stop. It startled her when, after a short pause during which he remained buried inside her, he began fucking her again. The only difference was a slight softness. And after a couple of minutes he was as hard as ever. God the man could fuck. It seemed that cumming had been a way to settle in; now he was getting down to business.

His hands and mouth were all over her. He teased and touched and licked and nibbled. He kissed her passionately, sucking her tongue into his mouth, thrusting his into hers. He nuzzled her ears, nipping the lobes. He kissed her neck. And sucked her nipples, licking her breasts. He was like a starving man who'd stumbled across a free buffet. He wasn't about to leave any part untasted.

And his hands. Caressing and clenching, running over every inch of exposed skin. Clutching her shoulders as he tried to thrust deeper and deeper. Cupping and squeezing her large pliant breasts. Plucking the nipples. Grasping the cheeks of her ass. It made her feel wanted in a way she'd never known before. It was obvious he couldn't get enough of her body.

And through all the kissing and licking and touching he was fucking. Trying different angles and new motions. Fast and hard one minute and then the next he was moving soft and slow. And he kept going. Like that battery bunny on speed. She wasn't sure how much more she could stand.

JAKE DIDN'T HEAR HER at first. He was too caught up in reveling in the sensations he'd been missing for so long. He loved everything about her body. She was so soft, and warm, and wet, and welcoming. She'd hooked her heels behind his knees. And when she was close to cumming she'd grab his butt and pull him into her. Moaning. Wailing with a lust drenched voice. He'd lost track of how many times she'd cum.

"You're starting to hurt me," she said, apparently not for the first time. "Hey. It hurts."

This time she got through. He stopped and looked down at her face.

"You're rubbing my pussy raw," she said. "It hurts."

Jake felt torn. He didn't want to stop; this was feeling too good. He was ready to fuck until the last ding dong of doom clanged and faded. But he didn't want to hurt her either. He was starting to like her a lot. Up to this point, once she'd gotten past her first fears, she'd been with him all the way.

"I love the way you're fucking me," she said. "I wish I could keep going but it hurts too much. I haven't been with anyone for awhile so I'm tender."

He looked at her, feeling a little angry. He was almost ready to start again even if it made her scream with pain. Then he had an idea.

"Turn over," he said as he abruptly pulled out and sat back on his heels.

"What?" She said.

"Turn over, goddamnit." With a look of confusion she rolled over onto her belly. "Now lift up your ass. Yeah, that's it. A little higher."

DARLENE REALIZED WHAT he was planning to do the

115

moment he pushed into her cunt and filled his fingers with the slickness of his semen and her own lubrication and began spreading it over her rectum. Pressing two fingers in.

"Oh yeah, I love to be fucked in the ass," she sighed, feeling the familiar pain that she knew would soon turn to pleasure.

"That's good because that's what you're going to get whether you like it or not," he said.

He sounded mean but his fingers made sure she was ready for his cock. And then she felt the head of it sliding in. It felt so big. He pushed in further and her asshole began making its adjustment, she gritted her teeth at the discomfort. Then he was fucking her. Sliding slowly back and forth.

"Shit yeah," he grunted. "I should have thought of this earlier. Your tight little asshole is going to make me cum again. My balls have needed to be emptied like this for a long long time."

"Oh. Oh. Oh," she was moaning with every inward thrust. The hurting was gone now. She was feeling the kindling heat that would in time become the volcanic core of orgasm.

They continued for some time. Making little grunts and moans of pleasure. He began thrusting harder and faster. "Oh yeah," he said. "I can feel it coming. I'm going to dump my cum deep inside your fucking ass."

The heat was building inside her. He'd been rubbing his hands over her back and ass, grabbing handfuls of her cheeks. Now he was leaning down and cupping her swinging breasts, catching her nipples in his fingers and pulling them.

"Oh yes, yes," she moaned. "I'm going to cum too."

This seemed to excite him and he moved even more powerfully. Driving his hard cock deep inside her ass. He was still pulling her nipples.

"Play with your clitty," he said. "Make yourself cum. I want to feel you cum. Make your asshole all tight around my cock."

She reached between her breasts and found her rigid clit. She felt the heat become a torrent. "Oh, I'm going to cum. Oh yes, fuck me. Don't stop."

He was pounding into her now. Making loud inarticulate sounds.

And then it was as if burning lava was filling her body. Hot and satisfying. "Oh God yes, Oh God," she was crying out.

"I'm cumming, Oh God, I'm cumming."

He dropped her breasts and grabbed her shoulders. Slamming into her. Pulling her asshole down around the base of his cock. Then, once more, he screamed like a wild animal. She felt him pulsing inside her. And felt the hot liquid flow. He jerked several times and went limp on top of her. His cock dwindled and then popped out. She could feel his cum oozing out of her.

"Oh shit. Oh fuck," he said, flopping over on his back beside her. "Oh sweet Jesus, I've needed that for so long. Goddamn that felt good."

They lay inert, breathing heavily, for what seemed like hours.

She turned her head to look at him. "I have a little proposition," she said. He swiveled his head to return her gaze. "You can stay in my house. That's my part of the bargain."

"You don't want to do that," he said.

"Yes, I do."

"No you don't."

"I know who you are. You're Jake Barlow."

He looked stunned. "And you let me fuck you knowing that?"

She laughed, feeling the sore ache of satisfaction in both her holes. "Yeah right. And if I'd asked you not to would you have stopped?"

"No, probably not," he said with a short laugh, looking as contrite as she imagined it was possible for him. "So what's my part of the bargain?"

"Use me. Fuck me any way, any time, and any place you want to."

He stared at her. For a moment she thought he might refuse. He turned his head and looked into the sky. "Only a fool would turn down an offer like that. And my mama didn't raise no fool."

"Deal?" She asked.

"Deal," he said.

She felt a rush of warmth fill her belly. And, incredibly, saw that he was getting hard again.

"Roll over," he said.

"Jake, I'm sore."

"Shut the fuck up and roll over."

She did what she was told, feeling anxious. He got to his knees beside her, stuffing his fingers into her pussy. Then he was rubbing the thick goo he found there between her breasts.

"I think it's time you got a good titty fucking," he said as he straddled her. "And got a mouthful of my baby juice."

She felt his rough hands pushing her breasts tight around his cock as he slid between them. She opened her mouth. Oh yes, she thought. This is going to be what they call a win/win situation.

She's Bound To Be Pleased

It had begun in the morning when he'd handed her a dress she'd never seen before and asked her to wear it. This struck her as odd because he was more often interested in what she didn't wear than in what she did. But she was glad to do it if it would please him. And it was a nice dress, long and flowing with a print of twining bright green vines and brilliant yellow flowers. Remembering his second request she didn't put on a bra or panties. When she entered the kitchen where he sat drinking his coffee she could clearly read the approval and admiration in his eyes.

"I've got some errands to run," he said. "I'll be back around two. Don't make any plans for the afternoon."

As he made his way to the door he took her in his arms and gave her a warm hug. She felt his hands pull up the dress and clench her smooth bare cheeks. "Good girl," he said, kissing her and giving her bottom a goodbye swat.

She knew him well enough to know that something was up, probably of an erotic nature. She moved around the house doing her chores and anticipated the pleasures to come. She could feel the petals of her soft flower swell and bloom, gracing the air with the scent of their aromatic dew.

He returned a little after two but acted as if the earlier conversation had never happened, going out to the garage to putter around, and then disappearing into his office. She was unable to sit still as she wondered what was going to happen and when. Around three she heard his cell phone chime and the low mumble of his voice as he spoke to someone. About ten minutes later he emerged from his office and gave her a sign to follow him as he walked toward the bedroom.

"Lie down," he said, gesturing towards the bed. She leaned back and she saw him reach down and pick up the end of one of the soft restraints. In short order she found herself tied to the bed with her arms and legs spread but her body covered by the colorful dress. He opened the top drawer of the nightstand and pulled out a blindfold which he proceeded to tie around her head in a way that closed off any view of her surroundings. Now, only able to use her ears, she tried to follow his movements around the room. First the CD player began playing soft sensual music. And then she heard a match being struck and moments later smelled a lavender scented candle. There was a soft plopping noise she took to be the sound of his clothes dropping into a chair. After that, for several long minutes, she could hear him walking around but couldn't tell what he was doing. The doorbell rang.

She assumed that he'd be alarmed but soon sensed that he was not. In fact, as far as she could tell, he walked to the front door without putting on any of his clothes. She could hear the door open and low voices speaking and then the footsteps of two people coming towards the bedroom. Her heart began racing and pounding in her ears like the drumming of a wild rhythm. Excitement and fear rushed through her body. For several long moments she was in a place where there was only fear. And no trust. Yet she did not speak. Her breathing was rapid as she tried to get the thoughts and feelings under some kind of control. And then there was the moment of surrender. The moment when she gave herself to him, and to the experience he was offering her. She inhaled deeply. And as she exhaled some of the tension left her body. Anticipation shuddered through her. Now, once again aware, she listened carefully, trying to determine if the stranger (or friend?) was a man or woman. All she heard was the sound of more clothes dropping.

Then, abruptly, someone climbed onto the bed, kneeling between her legs, and tore the dress up the middle, pulling it away from her body. She knew that her full large breasts and smooth shaven vulva were revealed to him and to the stranger. She felt helpless and exposed. Neither he nor the stranger made a sound but she could feel their eyes on her, gazing on every private part. And then fingertips lightly touched the inside of her thigh. Her nerves were so taut that she jerked and gasped loudly. But as the fingers continued to softly caress her skin she relaxed and opened herself to the sensations. A moment later different hands were touching her breasts and a mouth covered hers. She opened her mouth to accept the kiss and she felt a moustache touch her upper lip. Her first thought was that it must be her man. She responded with passion and then realized that other men have moustaches too. There was an instant in which she considered pulling back but that instant passed and she gave herself fully.

The hands between her legs continued their gentle dance but it soon became clear that the one spot they avoided was the spot that most ached to be touched. Each time they moved close to her pussy she'd lift her hips and then moan with frustration as she felt them skitter away. The man near her head was now kissing and nibbling at her neck as he rubbed his chest against her breasts. She was pretty sure it was her man but there was still a lingering doubt. Suddenly, after long long minutes of teasing, the fingers down below slipped up between her inner lips and circled around her clit a couple of times, thrilling her mound with an electric tingling. This had been so hungered for that she cried out and lifted her bottom off the bed, trying to follow the fingers as they pulled away. Apparently some signal had been given because all at once she was alone on the bed. She could hear two pairs of bare feet walking towards the kitchen accompanied by murmurs and quiet laughter. Her body ached to be touched again.

She heard talking and the refrigerator door open and close. A few minutes later it opened and closed again. A single pair of footsteps approached her. For a moment there was silence and she imagined the person looking at her spread eagle nakedness. Without warning something very cold touched her left nipple and circled her areola; it made her inhale sharply. And then, while the same cold object (a piece of ice, she assumed, because she could feel a cold rivulet sliding down her breast) was applied to her right nipple and areola, a warm mouth and tongue covered the left one. Back and forth, cold and warm, went the cold object and the warm mouth. She heard the other person enter the room and climb up between her legs. A cool liquid drizzled down on her open vulva. The other mouth began licking the unknown substance off and out of her pussy, making soft smacking noises. She was floating on a cushion of sensual stimulation. The person at her breasts got up and straddled her chest and spent several seconds performing some activity. Then the soft sticky head of a cock was pressed against her lips. She opened her mouth, took it in, and tasted honey. The man above her bent over and braced his arms. His hairy balls rubbed across her chest and she could feel his thighs against her breasts. He was moving himself back and forth inside her mouth, while making soft moaning sounds. She knew it wasn't her man. And, as if he was aware that she'd realized that she was with two men, she felt her man's cock slide into her very well lubricated vagina.

From this point on time was no longer linear. Her consciousness was expressed in shifting kaleidoscopic shards of feeling. Her body seemed to melt and flow out into space. Every square millimeter of the surface of her skin, every pore, every orifice, was now open to savor the next pattern of reality. Fear had vanished into infinity. She was the essential woman now, surrendered to the cosmos.

As he entered her he began to talk although the other man didn't speak. "You are so wet, sweetie," he said. "Oh yes, milk my cock." He moved inside her with long, firm, unhurried strokes.

"You're going to love this," he said, speaking to the other man. "She can squeeze your cock in a way you won't believe." The stranger's response was a moan as he withdrew from her mouth and her man pulled out of her cunt. She could feel them changing places and, as the stranger's cock buried itself in her pussy, her man's, wet with her lubrication, was pushing against her lips.

"Squeeze him, Baby," her man said, "show him what you can do." The stranger gave a loud groan as she complied.

"Oh yes, lick your hot juice off my cock," her man exclaimed. "Taste yourself." Reaching behind his thighs he found her hard nipples and began teasing and pulling them.

"Are you hot now, Baby?" he asked. "Do you like the way he's fucking you?" All she could do was nod which pushed the head of his cock to the back of her mouth. "Do you like his hard cock deep inside you?" She nodded again, moaning. Her hips jerked to meet his thrusts.

They changed places again. This time she was aware of some of the differences between them. The stranger's method of eating her was more delicate and tentative, almost feathery, and in some ways more exciting. His cock was longer than her man's and reached deeper inside her. But her man's was thicker and gave her more of a sense of fullness. Both of them felt good. And the stranger's smell, as he presented the wet head of his cock to her mouth, was sweetened by the scent of cologne. Her man's smell was muskier. Her man resumed his long unhurried strokes and she realized that the stranger moved quicker, more urgently.

Several minutes later her man withdrew and replaced his cock with two fingers. "Oh, you are so hot now, Baby." he said. "You are gushing. You like to be fucked by two men, don't you? You like having two hard cocks to play with?"

She felt him find her g-spot and begin rubbing. Three of his big fingers were inside her. And then four. She could hear the squishing sound of her wetness as he twisted them. She bucked her hips to keep them inside. The feeling from her g-spot, radiating through her belly, was like a low drawn out note of a cello, fierce and resonant. Then suddenly, once more, both men were gone, walking towards the kitchen. This time, powerfully aroused, she lay panting.

"Do you want anything to drink, honey?" her man asked. She hadn't even heard him come in.

"Some water, please."

He went out and came back, lifting her head to help her drink. Some of the water went down her chin and onto her chest. She felt him lick it up and then kiss her tenderly. "You sure seem to be having fun, sweetheart," he said. She gave him a huge smile.

She was now familiar with the pattern of intense stimulation and complete withdrawal that had been established. She didn't know how much time had passed but sensed that it had been at least a couple of hours. Neither the unknown man nor her man showed any signs of tiring. And her body sang with the delight of being the focus of so much loving attention. She anticipated the pleasures to come.

In contrast to what had gone before, the next period of activity was like whispers after shouting. They had settled on either side of her and then a cool breeze of delicate fabric brushed over her skin. One would move up her leg while the other would flow across her breasts. Or they both would waft up her thighs, over her open vulva, and across her belly. Gone for a moment, they'd then touch down somewhere else. In addition, there were gentle rain of random kisses on her lips, her neck, her breasts, and her inner thighs. She felt the entire surface of her body become sensitized. A tongue licked her nipple and the mouth blew air across it, making her gasp and shiver. Something brushed across her clitoris and then was gone. The fabric slid across her face and upper chest. Fingertips glided up her inner thigh. This went on and on, the passionate caresses of a ghost, until this too ended.

When the two men returned from their visit to the kitchen they climbed up on the bed near her head and, once they'd raised her up on a couple of pillows, dangled their cocks in her face. One was soft and the other half hard. She alternated between them, sucking and licking, feeling their ball sacks rub against her chin. Once the one of them who was half hard became erect he moved from her head to between her legs and entered her with a low moan. After moving back and forth a few times he withdrew and brought his cock, slick with her cream, to her mouth. Now, again, she had two hard cocks to lick and suck. It was exciting for her to experience two cocks at once, to sample how each one felt in her mouth, the textures, the tastes, and the smells. And then the man on the other side of her took a turn at fucking her and bringing her his cream drenched cock. Back and forth they went, fucking her and then bringing her juice on a stick. All the while they did this they were playing with her breasts and hard nipples. Then came another pause.

One of the men came into the room and she heard the drawer of her nightstand open and close. The telltale buzz of a vibrator filled the room. The sound moved down between her legs and as it entered her she could tell it was her Panther and Pearls vibe that was being worked into her cunt. Then there was a mouth at each of her nipples, sucking, licking, and nipping. Four hands roamed all over her body from her face and neck, down over her chest and tummy, down to her knees. From time to time one of the mouths would leave her breast to kiss her lips or kiss and nibble her neck and then return to her hard nipple. Occasionally one of the hands would slide the vibrator in and out a few times and press the panther against her clitoris. Once again, as she felt the first stirrings of orgasm, most of the stimulation ceased. The vibrator, however, was turned to the lowest speed setting and left inside the mouth of her pussy. It was excruciating to feel herself right on the edge with the vibrator maintaining her arousal.

"Okay Baby," she heard her man say. "It's time for the grand finale."

Hands pulled the vibrator out, turned it off, and then untied the restraints but kept tight hold of her wrists and ankles. She felt totally controlled. She was flipped over on her stomach. The restraints were retied but looser than before. Someone straddled her and pulled her up by her middle until she was on her hands and knees. A moment later the other man was sliding under her and arranging himself between her legs; she was aware of the man on top facilitating things and then the bottom man's cock was sliding into her wet pussy. Both she and the man inside her sighed simultaneously and she heard the top man respond. The bottom man pulled her head down to kiss her with his hot lips, sucking her tongue into his mouth hungrily, moaning.

"Fuck him," her man commanded from above. "Ride his hard cock with your juicy hot cunt. Make him come." She began rocking, feeling the hard cock slide in and out of herself. "Oh yeah." her man said from behind her. "That is so hot. You're getting your pussy cream all over his balls. God, your big ass looks so gorgeous on his fat cock. Fuck that motherfucker you hot cunt."

His words were filling her with a rich sexual fire. She and the stranger were fucking faster and harder. "Ride that hard motherfucker you horny cunt. Make him blow his load deep in your creamy pussy," she could hear him yelling. All the stimulation of this long afternoon, and now night, was rumbling over her like the frenetic tumult of a summer thundershower. It was almost frightening to feel the power of it building. She was panting in the darkness behind the blindfold. She could feel her breasts swinging wildly.

"Get ready Baby," she heard her man cry. "You're gonna get two cocks at once you gorgeous cunt." There was a moment of activity behind her and all at once her pussy was being stretched wide. She'd never felt so full. And the idea that she was now being fucked by two men in her pussy hole at once flashed through her. The gigantic storm came crashing down with full-bodied waves of orgasm. She'd never felt anything like this before in her life. Nothing so intense. A wild rainbow of colors danced through her consciousness. So much stimulation for so long had touched depths she never knew existed. She heard herself screaming as wave after cataclysmic wave of pleasure poured through her shuddering body. Her men too were shouting hoarsely. And then it subsided. The pounding waves slid away. The three of them were piled together like sacks of wet blankets on a deserted beach. None of them could move.

"I'm getting crushed under here," the bottom man gasped finally. Her man flopped off her back onto the bed next to her so she could lift herself up enough for the stranger to scuttle out. He didn't go far. The three of them lay in a deep daze for an unknown length of time. Dozing. At last the stranger gathered himself together and began putting on his clothes. When he was done her man walked him to the door and, after a short low conversation, he was gone. Her man returned and removed the restraints and blindfold. She lay there exhausted, feeling the wetness of her thighs and the come oozing out. He sat beside her with his hand on her belly.

"Who was that?" she asked at long last.

He looked down at her. "Somebody you know. Somebody you see quite often. You're going to have to guess which one."

She knew this was going to change the way she looked at the men who moved through her life from now on. And felt a thrilling spasm deep inside her cunt.

Hair Lover

Annie, my wife, and I met in college. I've always been a bit of a geek (that's what she calls me) and shy around women. But from the moment I saw her talking with a couple of her friends in the student union I knew I had to get to know her better.

What first caught my eye was how small she was. And then I was struck by the beauty of her face, surrounded by a mass of rich red-brown curls. Finally, what clinched it was the sense of impish vitality that seemed to emanate from her like heat off a radiator. Once, as I sat staring at her, she turned and looked straight into my eyes. I felt as if I'd been hit by lightning, so powerful was her presence. In the merest instant it seemed we each downloaded several gigabytes of information. And then she turned back to her friends.

It took awhile before much else happened. I was, as I said, a shy person. But slowly, like magnets drawn into each other's influence, we moved closer and closer throughout the next couple of weeks. And then we clicked. I learned later that she'd had her eye on me even before I'd seen her at the student union. It was all a cat and mouse game. And she, quite clearly, had been the cat.

We realized, even at the start, that we had very different approaches to interacting with the world and for a long time this made us both wonder if our relationship was, in fact, workable. But over the years we developed an understanding of how we complemented each other and came to respect and value our differences.

Annie is the adventurous one, the seeker, the swashbuckler, the spunky sprite, the bold zephyr; I'm the ballast, the keel, the counterweight, the appreciator. I play Sancho Panza to her Don Quixote. After many long talks we've come to the conclusion that she expresses and instigates feelings that I carry within myself but don't yet feel comfortable acting on while I give her a sense of safety because she knows that if things get too crazy I'll be clear-headed enough to put the brake on. Over the years we've developed a delicate, and delightfully vivid, balance between her style of being and mine to the profound enhancement of both our lives.

One of Annie's habits that threatened the stability of our early years was her openness to enjoying the attention of other men, especially when this included their intimate attention as well. She never made a secret of her other friendships and sexual dalliances and never apologized for them either. Her attitude was that it was her body and she could do with it what she would and if I couldn't handle her choices I could move on. It wasn't that she didn't understand my insecurities or empathize with the hurt I felt but, despite her real concern, she refused to be bound by my limitations.

And she didn't (and doesn't) maintain a double standard. She encouraged me to experience other women which, because of my diffidence, sometimes took the form of covert facilitation.

Eventually, as the true depth of her love and respect for me became clear, I began to appreciate and even delight in the gift of freedom she offered me. I never evolved into what anyone would call a womanizer but I liked knowing that if an interaction with a woman reached the point where sexual intimacy seemed like a good idea I could act on it without guilt. Another benefit was the quality of honesty it built between us. Our relationship progressed and slowly I felt less and less of a need to hide what I thought and felt because I learned that although she might express hurt, anger or irritation she was always willing to work through these emotions till we both knew where we stood. And, in time, through a rather long and painful process, I taught myself to do the same for her.

Several months after we first became sexually intimate, during the pillow talk following an open and tender evening of love-making, with more than a little trepidation I broached the subject of my interest in women with a lot of body hair. Her initial reaction, as I had feared, was one of amused incredulity; she couldn't imagine how a man could be aroused by a woman with hairy armpits and legs.

Annie, I should say, was an unconventional young woman. She didn't wear much make-up. The pieces of jewelry she chose tended to be understated and selected more to express something about herself than for ostentation. And, although she had a marvelous sense of style, her clothing was simple and inexpensive. But one thing she did, religiously, was shave her armpits and legs.

So, even though she'd had some experience with the tastes of a variety of men, the idea that a man could find hair on a woman to be sexually stimulating struck her as foreign. But as I talked about my feelings and the moments in my life in which my fascination had been revealed to me, even as my fingers played in the reddish-brown fluff of her pussy, it began to dawn on her how deep my feelings went.

When, finally, I summoned up all my courage and asked her if she'd stop shaving for me all she would say was, "I'll think about it." I knew her well enough by then to know that I would have to be content with that answer as there was no point in pushing her.

A couple of months later I found that a soft russet fuzz was beginning to adorn her legs and the pockets under her arms. At first, not wishing to raise my expectations, I told myself that she was taking a break from shaving. But then one night, since a couple of weeks had passed and the fuzz continued to flourish, as I knelt between her open legs slowly thrusting and withdrawing while stroking the new furry down on her calves, I asked her if she had, in fact, stopped wielding her razor.

"Yes," she said sweetly.

"Thank you Darling," I whispered, leaning down to take her in my arms, "I love you."

It was a special moment for both of us.

Annie wasn't, however, a hirsute woman. She developed a couple of pleasant copper colored patches under her arms but the hair on her legs never went beyond a soft reddish down while the fur on her pussy never extended farther than the small neat triangle bounded by her thighs and the bottom of the swell of her belly.

At the time that this story begins Annie and I had been together for nine years. We'd graduated from college, settled in the Northwest, and both started our own businesses. I am a freelance computer programmer and consultant and Annie owns and operates a small printing firm. For several years we'd concentrated, almost exclusively, on building up our businesses but now things were beginning to settle down and we were casting around for new worlds to explore.

As usual this adventure came about as a result of Annie's explorations. It started with her telling me about some people who'd come into the printing shop; she described them as "interesting", "different" and said, "I think you'd like them". But when she told me she'd been invited to a gathering by some of her new friends I was less than overcome by the idea of tagging along. And even the tepid interest I did have cooled when she went out and bought a large used tent, quantities of prime surplus store camping gear, and informed me that this gathering entailed transporting this equipment to a forested area several hours away and creating a livable(?) habitation. I liked nature. But I tended to prefer to experience it through a picture window or through the windshield of an automobile.

As the date of the gathering approached I began to feel a subtle but mounting pressure from Annie. It puzzled me because she and I didn't insist that one share the other's pet project if there was a lack of interest. At the time I put it down to her enthusiasm.

One day, unable to guarantee my presence at the gathering by less direct means, she happened to mention with elaborate casualness that her friends called themselves Wylde Wymyn and, as part of their acceptance of their bodies, refused to shave their legs and armpits. They also, she recollected, were casual about nudity and enjoyed going about "skyclad", which was the term they used.

In the merest fraction of a nanosecond I was totally committed to being at that place even if I had to pack the tent and all the attendant doodads on my back. My imagination grew so inflamed that I couldn't detach from my fantasies enough to wonder what her motivation for telling me this might be. Upon reflection, after the fact, it was clear that she'd conceived a plan that had been in motion for awhile. But that revelation was several weeks away from dawning.

Now I was the one who found it hard to contain my impatience at the ambling pace of time. Annie must have treasured many moments of private amusement at the sight of my obsessive glances at the calendar and frantic fingerings of the magic date. Visions of thickly furred shanks, armpits and pussies danced through my head.

At last the big day arrived. We'd packed the car the night before, stuffing the trunk and backseat to the point of maximum density, so all we had to do was get dressed, drink a few quick cups of coffee, and head for the freeway as the sun came peeking over the mountains. The anticipation of adventure, of the opening out of new possibilities, put me in a euphoric mood. I looked at Annie and saw the same deep glow in her face. I felt a strong rush of emotion.

"I love you," I said, reaching out to take her hand.

She turned and looked into my eyes. "I love you too, sweetheart. Very, very much."

I turned back to the road to hide my overflowing feelings and felt her squeeze my hand.

We arrived at the site of the gathering several hours later, about 10:00 a.m. It was being held on someone's private property and, following the directions we'd been given, we turned off the main highway onto a narrow gravel road bounded by a thick growth of trees and drove down it for what seemed like an hour. At one point we met a carload of people coming out and had to negotiate a careful pass with two tires on the road and two tires off. They waved as they went by and we waved back. We came to a place where there was a small yellow tent set up in a small grassy area beside the road. A tall shirtless young man with a scraggly Van Dyke clambered out of the tent as we approached, bearing a clipboard which held a thick sheaf of papers. After asking our names he flipped through the papers until he found the one he needed, made a few notations, slipped a green card under our windshield wiper, and waved us on. We drove for another couple of minutes until, making a turn, we found ourselves facing a large meadow surrounded by trees. We could see that the road ran around the circumference of the meadow and there was an arrow pointing to the right. A hundred yards away a large olive green tent was set up beside the road and a small number of people were moving around underneath. As we came up to the tent a dark-haired, bare-breasted, woman in red shorts detached herself from the activity, picked up several sheets of paper off a small table, and walked up to my side of the car. I felt Annie's knee touch mine as the woman greeted us with a smile and bent down to hand me the papers which, she explained, contained the rules of conduct and a map of the area. I knew Annie had seen, as I had, that thick black tufts of hair were peeking out from under the woman's arms and her legs were covered with dark hair.

"I think I'm going to like this," I told Annie as we drove away, headed for what Darla, the finely furred woman, had said was the main camping place.

"Yes, Darling, I think you will," she said. There was something in her tone that made me look at her quizzically but all I saw was a sweet blank smile of impenetrable innocence.

We spent the next three hours erecting the tent and arranging the various pieces of camping equipment that Annie had purchased into some semblance of a living space. Annie was no more of an outdoorsperson than I was so we both contracted severe cases of irritability caused by the frustration of wrestling with unfamiliar materials. I'm being only faintly facetious when I say that the stress of trying to figure out how to set up the tent almost ended our marriage. But we managed to work out most of the kinks and find a place for everything.

There'd been four tents set up when we arrived and three new groups had appeared since. There was a quiet sense of camaraderie but everyone was focusing on their own tasks. So when we finished preparing our temporary home Annie announced, with some acerbity due to her irritableness, that she was going to walk down to the big tent and see if they needed any help. I'd glanced at the map and noticed that there was a place called the "Old Swimming Hole" that I thought bore looking into. If anyone was going to take off their clothes I felt it was safe to assume that this would be the spot.

I found the path indicated on the map and followed its rocky way down a slope through a forest of evergreens until I came to a small river. The path turned right and ran along the edge of the river and after I'd proceeded along the path for about two hundred yards it brought me to a place where there'd been some effort made to excavate the rocks to deepen the riverbed. To the right there was an open grassy area. I knew I'd found the "Old Swimming Hole". The problem was that I was alone.

For about half an hour I sat on a rock and watched the river slide by until I got restless and took the path back to the camping area. I spent the rest of the afternoon sitting at my trusty Toshiba portable computer rewriting an instruction manual for a client and watching for nudity in the swelling flow of people arriving to set up their temporary living quarters. It was, I found, very pleasant to key in a sentence or two and then be able to look up and see a naked woman, or man, for that matter, pounding in tent stakes or catch sight of a bare-breasted woman walking up or down the road. At first, I'll admit, I felt a sexual thrill at the sight. I'd never been in a situation where nudity was accepted with so little fanfare. But as the afternoon wore on my feelings changed from focused sexual response to a more general appreciation. On a level I couldn't quite put my finger on I felt a deep tension draining out of me.

I hadn't seen so many unshaven women in one place since I was in college. And I'd never seen so many naked women with thickly furred armpits and hairy legs.

The sun was dipping behind the trees across the meadow when I looked up from the computer screen to see a small, red-haired, bare-breasted woman in jeans walking up the road with her shirt and bra dangling from her hand and realized, with a start, that it was Annie.

"Becoming a nudist, I see," I said as she walked up; she seemed to be dancing with suppressed energy.

"Oh Mark. I love this," she said as she dropped her shirt and bra on the table beside the computer, took the sides of my face in her hands, and gave me a passionate kiss. I reached up to stroke both sides of her ribcage. A moment later she broke away, patting my head, and ducked into the tent. Before I could recover she popped out again, naked. "God. This makes me feel so free," she practically sang and pranced over to perch on my lap. Reaching around her I shut down the computer and we talked about our experiences and impressions since we'd parted.

Annie told me that she'd been assisting Darla and the men and women of the kitchen crew as they prepared the evening meal. She described how she'd watched the reactions of those passing by to Darla and the other semi-nude women and was struck, as I had been, by the lack of awkward sexual responses. So she decided to try it herself. She caught a few appreciative glances from a couple of the men but on the whole nothing changed. What surprised her was how she felt, the sense of relaxation and freedom.

Shortly after I told her the story of my little trek to the "Old Swimming Hole" Annie looked at her watch and announced that it was time to eat. By now the sun had dipped down into the tops of the trees and groups of people were straggling down the road towards the big tent. Annie slipped into one of my old t-shirts while I gathered together our plates, cups and silverware, and we joined the procession.

The food, all vegetarian, was laid out buffet style and as we went through the line Annie pointed out the dishes that she'd worked on.

Once our plates were full she led me to one of the less populated tables and settled us down across from two young women who were already seated. We sat down and I realized from the way they smiled at her that they knew Annie. I noticed a peculiar speculative look in the eyes of the woman with long black hair in front of me. I assumed this was due to curiosity about "Annie's husband". She had a rich olive complexion, dark eyes and full lips; she was wearing a large t-shirt but it was evident that she was large breasted and wasn't wearing a bra.

"Mark, these are two of my friends. This is Heather," she said, with a gesture toward the dark-haired woman." And this is Cassie" Annie continued, indicating the other woman.

"Nice to meet you," the second woman said as she took my hand. I felt a little thrill of pleasure as I gazed into her large smiling hazel eyes framed by fluffy shoulder-length light brown hair. She was wearing a colorful dress that was tight enough to reveal that she was slim without being skinny.

As we ate the three women chatted. Occasionally Annie would elicit a comment from me but for the most part I listened and observed. It became evident that these two were regular patrons of my wife's printshop and seemed to know her quite well.

Ever since adolescence I've been the type of man whose response to women is so powerful that the force of my feelings hogties my tongue and, often, my brain as well. I am like a pilgrim struck dumb by the wonder of God. Over the years I've learned to become more detached and have developed a sort of clumsy flirtatiousness but in the depths of my heart I feel the same feeling of speechless awe. This was my general state of mind as I listened to the three women talk.

We remained at the table long after the others had finished eating and talked about a variety of subjects. I grew more comfortable and began to contribute more to the conversation. By the end of the evening we were all feeling pretty chummy. At last Heather stood up and announced that she, for one, needed to get some sleep. She was wearing shorts and I couldn't help but notice the rich growth of black hair on her legs. My cock stirred into a partial erection. She turned to go and my eyes also took in the fullness of her bottom. Cassie rose as well and said goodnight.

"Do you like my friends?" Annie asked me as we walked back to the tent.

"Yeah, I do," I said, putting my arm around her shoulders and pulling her close. She slipped her arm around my waist and gave me a sweet squeeze.

"Do you think they're attractive"

I stopped in the middle of the road and tried to see her face in the darkness. "What are you getting at?"

"I'm curious, honey, that's all." Once more I heard that tone of opaque innocence.

"Yeah, I do," I said, pulling her against me, running my hands down her body, and then sliding them up under the shirt. The slightly cool softness of her bottom under my fingertips was very arousing.

"I'm glad," she said as her lips found mine and her belly ground against my cock. We kissed passionately, our bodies fitting together, knowing that we were sharing an idea. Occasionally, throughout the years, we'd talked and fantasized about what it would be like to invite another woman or man to join our lovemaking. We'd never done this but there had been times when we'd developed detailed fantasies about one or another of our acquaintances. It seemed to me that Annie was using the fact of Heather's hairiness to add some extra spice to our little game.

"Let's get to the tent," she said breathlessly, pushing me back. Hand in hand we practically ran all the way.

Unzipping the door and tumbling in, Annie whipped off the t-shirt and was naked. It took me a bit longer, since I had jeans on as well as a t-shirt, but not much. In an instant we were lying on the bedding with our bodies pressed together in sweet naked glory. I slid my hand down her side, over the little swell of her belly, and then slid a finger into the mouth of her pussy. I was surprised to discover she was quite moist.

"Oh baby, I'm ready; put it in." She whispered.

I didn't need any more encouragement. A second later the soft slick heat of her pussy was hugging the shaft of my cock.

"Oh yes, oh God yes." She sighed.

I put my left arm around her shoulders, pushed my right hand under her bottom, and began moving inside her with firm insistent strokes. She kissed my neck and chin and then found my mouth with a passionate hunger. Our tongues tangled in a desperate dance, striving for connection. I could feel her chest vibrating with low, barely audible, moans.

She pulled away and whispered in my ear. "Would you like to fuck Heather, baby? Would you like to see her hairy cunt? Would you like that?" Her words had the effect she intended; I began moving into her with a deep urgent need. "Oh yeah. Oh fuck me, baby. Fuck me the way you'd fuck Heather's hairy pussy." I didn't last long. In less than a minute of frantic thrusting I buried the full length of my cock inside her and loosed my seed in three exquisite spurts.

Maintaining the connection while kissing her neck and face I reached down between us and began to massage the area around her clitoris with my fingers.

"Your turn, sweetheart," I whispered, "I wanna feel you come." I bent down to lick the sweat-salt off her little breasts and suck each long nipple into my mouth. Then I lifted my head and, after kissing her mouth, asked, "Would you like to see me fuck Heather, baby?"

"Yes, yes I want to see that," she said. "I want to see your cock fucking her hairy cunt. Yes, ah, ahh, ahhh." I felt her tummy trembling under my hand. Then her body relaxed. I withdrew my semi-hard cock, lay down beside her, and put my arm around her shoulders as she moved over to settle her head on my chest. This is how we fell asleep.

Sometime in the night I awoke, as I often do, chasing some scrap of dreamthought into consciousness. Annie and I had shifted our positions and were now lying butt to butt. I lay listening to the night, trying to find my bearings in this unfamiliar place. It was then I heard the muted whimpering cries of a woman's pleasure. The warm flush of desire surged through my body. I wrapped my hand around the hard shaft of my cock and held myself. The cries continued for about half a minute and then subsided. Hearing the unknown woman made me realize how far sound carried in a village of cloth houses. I wondered how many people had heard Annie and me talking about Heather; it made me feel a little silly. Still holding myself I fell back to sleep. The next time I woke up it was daylight and Annie was preparing to leave the tent in last night's t-shirt and a pair of cut-off jeans. I could hear other people stirring outside.

"What time is it," I asked.

She came over and gave me a quick good-morning kiss before answering. "About six-thirty, hon; breakfast will be ready in another hour. You can probably get some coffee now though." With a little wave and a smile she disappeared out the door. I lay back, listening to the sounds of people moving around me and the quiet murmur of voices. It was odd to have the private and public spheres separated by a thin sheet of nylon fabric.

After awhile I rose and, like Annie, donned a pair of cut-offs and a t-shirt and ambled down to the dining tent. There were about fifteen people sitting around drinking coffee or tea and talking. Annie was busy making french toast so I got my own cup of coffee and sat on the outside of the circle and listened to the conversation. After about fifteen minutes Heather appeared and, after speaking to Annie for a couple of minutes, brought her cup of coffee over to sit beside me. She was wearing a long purple and black dress that was made out of a diaphanous, almost transparent, material. The fact that I could see the vague shapes of her large breasts shifting under the gauze and the shadow of her full pubic patch unnerved me. Somehow she seemed more naked than the nude women I'd seen yesterday. I was very aroused, especially after the fantasy session with Annie last night, but I didn't feel comfortable revealing this to Heather. However, adding to my distress, I had the distinct suspicion that Heather was well aware of my turmoil and was intentionally playing on my arousal. And succeeding. Even though we managed to maintain a mangled conversation our words conveyed the least of our communication.

At one point Annie came over and brought Heather and me each a plate piled with scrambled eggs, fried potatoes and French toast. She set the plates in front of us and I happened to catch the rather enigmatic glance that passed between them.

"You've got a very sweet husband," Heather said, placing her hand on my bare thigh and giving it a squeeze.

I felt flushed and flustered. I had an almost full erection that, because I'd been unable to adjust it, had snaked down the leg of my cut-offs and was threatening to stick its head out the bottom. I looked at Annie with a pleading expression. My dear wife headed back to the stove wearing the hint of a knowing smile.

I tried to focus my attention on eating but it was hard to concentrate with Heather's almost naked body so close by. I couldn't help but wonder what she'd look like without the dress on, what the true extent of her hairiness was. Annie had talked about Heather's "hairy cunt" last night but I didn't know if she was speaking of something she'd seen or was simply trying to excite me. I was hoping I'd get the chance to see for myself sometime during the weekend.

Even while I was entertaining these thoughts, and we ate, Heather and I continued to talk. She stopped being so flirtatious and the conversation deepened; I began to feel more at ease. I asked her about her involvement with the Wylde Wymyn and what it meant to her and, as she answered my questions, I realized that what I'd taken to be a kind of joke was in fact a disciplined search for life-sustaining values.

We finished eating and kept talking.

"What is the meaning of not shaving your legs and armpits?" I asked. She gave me a brief, but knowing, look of amusement and then became serious.

"I've felt for a long time that it's important for me to accept and respect the form my body naturally takes. This means, for me, accepting that I'm a big woman, what many would call fat; it also means accepting the fact that due to my genetic makeup my body sprouts great quantities of hair. I choose not to fight those things. But it's been hard. There have been people who've felt they had the right to say some pretty nasty things to me." There was a slight catch in her voice that I sensed indicated the presence of a hidden well of pain. "And yet, on the positive side, it moved me to seek out others who view life the same way I do. The poet Charles Simic puts it this way, 'He who cannot howl will never find his pack'. I've found my pack and I've never been happier in my life."

At some point Annie joined us with her own plate of food. Then

Cassie showed up. The conversation flowed off into directions that didn't interest me and I grew restive. One of the kitchen assistants came by looking for volunteers to help collect and haul the garbage and I offered my services. This occupied about an hour and a half.

It was about 10:30 when I got back to the tent. Annie was nowhere in sight and there was very little activity around the tents. After considering my options I decided to try my luck at the "Old Swimming Hole" again. Taking an old blanket and a book, A Guide for the Perplexed, I headed down the path I'd taken yesterday.

This time I was in luck. There was a small group of naked men and women splashing in the water and several children playing among the rocks at the river's edge. Feeling a little guilty about being here to watch the naked women I walked past them a ways and settled myself in the shade of a large evergreen whose lower branches had been lopped off. I sat looking around with my book in my hand pretending to be absorbing the marvels of nature, which I was, but I was more intent on catching glimpses of the naiads playing in the pool than the trees, rocks, and sky. All the women had dark patches under their arms.

After about fifteen minutes I began to feel increasingly conspicuous being the only one dressed. I've always been a modest person so the idea of taking off my own clothes was slow in forming. But finally, figuring that everyone else was naked so I might as well be naked too, I pulled off my t-shirt and slid out of my cutoffs. It was a peculiar sensation at first. To be exposed in a public setting, even if everyone else was exposed too. And yet, as I lay there, I began to feel the same deep sense of relaxation I'd felt yesterday afternoon. I became less focused on the people in the water and began to read my book. A couple of hours later the population in the pool had dwindled down to one couple sitting chest deep in the water gazing into each other's eyes. I decided, reluctantly, that my time could be better spent working on the training manual so I put on my cut-offs, gathered my things, and walked back up the path. I neared the tent and heard the pealing of female laughter. I pushed through the door and was greeted by the abrupt descent of conspiratorial silence. Heather and Cassie were sitting on two of our camp stools while Annie, naked, was stretched out on the bedding and leaning against a couple of cushions. Heather was wearing the same purple and black dress she'd been wearing earlier and Cassie had on a yellow cotton sundress. Each of them was holding a glass of white wine. They were looking at me and I felt an indefinable sense of tense expectation.

"Hi sweetheart," my wife said, "why don't you pour yourself some wine and join us?"

"What's going on?" I asked. I took the glass Annie handed me and tipped the jug to fill it. The three women giggled, a bit hysterically I thought.

"Oh, just having some girltalk," Heather said. I looked at each one of them in turn with growing suspicion. I couldn't imagine why they were acting this way, like little kids with a guilty secret.

"Annie, what's going on?" I asked again.

"Somebody's got to get this thing rolling," Heather said. I couldn't tell if she was talking to herself or to the two other women. I knew I wasn't the recipient. "And it might as well be me."

Annie and Cassie shifted and exchanged a brief glance. Cassie ran the palms of her hands down her thighs and then clasped her hands around her knee. I was mystified.

Heather spread her legs under the dress and put her hands on her knees." Annie says you like hairy women," she said, sliding her hands up her thighs with seductive deliberation until her dress was bunched up around her waist. "How do you like this?"

I felt as if I'd been slammed in the chest with a sledge hammer. My heart was beating and my mouth was dry. A hot flush spread across my face; I couldn't believe this was happening. I licked my lips and looked at Annie. She seemed to be enjoying my discomfiture. They all were. My gaze returned to Heather. She was the hairiest woman I'd seen in my life in or out of a magazine. Her legs were covered with a profusion of short black hair that dwindled somewhat past her knees but then burst forth in rich, curly, abundance around her pussy, spreading out over her inner thighs.

"Show him the rest of it," Annie said.

"I will if Cassie shows him hers," Heather said. We all turned to Cassie who flushed. She hesitated for a moment, stood up, and pulled her dress over her head. She, like Heather, wasn't wearing anything underneath her dress. I was beginning to recover from the shock of Heather's sudden exposure and so was able to focus my attention on Cassie a little better.

Cassie's hairiness was different, less dramatic, than Heather's. Her hair was a light brown, almost blond, and covered her lower body with a soft carpet of fuzz. She too had a thick pubic patch but only a narrow line of longer hairs climbed all the way to her navel. She made a teasing little turn, like a model at the end of a runway, lifted her arms and clasped her hands behind her head to show off the full growth under her arms.

At this point I had no idea how far this was meant to go or even if there was any kind of real understanding among the three of them. I knew that I was enjoying what I was seeing and if they were willing and Annie didn't mind I sure as hell wasn't going to complain.

"Your turn Heather," Cassie said, sitting down.

Heather stood up and pulled off her dress. She was what I'd describe as plump, not obese really, but well padded with large pendulous breasts tipped with dark areolas the size of mason jar lids and sporting thick nipples. Seeing her upright made me realize how bushy her bush truly was. The thick mass of hair rose in a pyramid to her navel with a few stragglers climbing past it. She, like Cassie, clasped her hands behind her head and did a flirtatious little bump and grind. Her armpits bristled with a long luxurious growth. There was even a small patch between her breasts and a number of curly hairs growing out of her areolas.

"Well, we're all naked. Why don't you join us," Cassie said.

"I, uhhh," I turned my eyes to Annie. I had a full erection I was sure she was aware of. The other two had probably seen it as well.

"Don't look at me," she said, "fair is fair."

It was beginning to sink in that the only limit here might be the sky. The idea was exciting, certainly, but it was also more than a little intimidating. Not only was the thought of satisfying three women daunting but I wasn't at all sure how Annie would handle the reality of seeing me with someone else. For one thing Annie was sensitive about the size of her breasts and, obviously, Heather was quite large; Cassie too, while much smaller than Heather, had bigger boobs than my darling wife. The notion of finding myself in the middle of an ugly scene didn't appeal to me at all. I was still looking into Annie's eyes.

"Everything is all right Mark, it truly is," Annie said. "This was my idea and Heather and Cassie were willing."

"An it harms none, do as you will," Heather said before turning and arranging her dress on a box next to the wall of the tent. I marveled at the sight of her full bottom and the hair that swarmed out of the crack of her butt and over the inner cheeks. Then, her large breasts swinging, she returned to the stool.

They were all watching me. I felt rather awkward and ridiculous but also excited by the feeling of suspense. This must be how a stripper feels, I thought. And, acting the part, I undid the top button and, holding the side together, slowly pulled down the zipper. It was funny to see the intentness on their faces, even

Annie who knew very well what was going to pop out. I turned around and wiggled my butt.

They got into the spirit of my little game and started calling for me to take it off. All off. I wrapped my t-shirt around my waist, slid my cut-offs down my legs, stepped out of them, and flung them in the air. The women laughed and clapped. Holding my t-shirt in front of me I turned around to face them and, with a sinking feeling, threw the t-shirt after the shorts.

I'd compared the size of my erect cock with enough of my boyhood friends to know that I was bigger than many and not as big as some. I didn't often worry. But to have three women avidly staring at that one part of my anatomy did make me a little anxious.

"Nice," said Cassie.

"Hmmm," Heather said.

"Come here, baby," my wife said, patting the bedding.

When I sat down beside her she put her hand on my chest and gently pushed me back till I was supine. "I don't think Mark will mind if you get better acquainted," Annie told them Heather eased off the stool and, dropping to her hands and knees, crawled towards me. Her nipples brushed my legs and thighs. At this point Annie leaned over and kissed me passionately, pushing her tongue into my mouth. Wet warmth enveloped the head of my cock and descended the shaft. A moment later I sensed someone, it had to be Cassie, settle down to my left and a hand began to rub my belly. I felt as if I was suspended in a warm bath of sensuality .

Annie pulled back and looked down at Heather. All that could be seen was a veil of long black hair moving up and down. Then Cassie bent down to kiss me. Her lips were cooler than Annie's and her kiss more tentative. I reached out and stroked her shoulder and back before sliding my hand around to cup her breast.

"Hmm," she hummed into my mouth. I caught her nipple with the tips of my fingers and gently tugged. "Hmmm," she said again. The tentativeness began to melt away as her kiss became more forceful. I felt her reach across me. Curious, I opened my eyes and turned them as far to the right as I could; I saw that she'd captured one of Annie's long nipples with her own fingertips. I gave the nipple in my fingertips a couple of sharp tugs and felt her laugh. I turned my eyes in time to see her do the same to Annie. Annie opened her eyes to look at us. I tugged Cassie's tit again and watched her tug Annie's. Annie reached out to give my nipple a hard pinch.

"Ouch." I said.

Cassie pulled away laughing and I felt Heather's mouth leave my cock. I glanced down to see her looking up with a quizzical smile, holding my gleaming cock upright in her hand. No one offered to explain why we were laughing so she went back to licking along the shaft. I looked at Annie and saw that her gaze was fixed on Cassie's face. Turning to Cassie I saw that she was looking at Annie with the same intent expression. A moment later they both leaned into me and their lips met above my chest. I was more than a little shocked; Annie had never expressed any explicit sexual interest in a woman before. She was expressing it now. I could see the passion sparking between them. I maneuvered my arms out of the tangle and moved them till I could stroke both their backs. But a moment later Annie was standing up and stepping across me as Cassie rolled over on her back. In another second they were in each other's arms. I was astounded.

At this point Heather grew tired of sucking my cock. She got up and reached into a pocket in her dress, pulled out a condom, and knelt beside me to roll it on. Then she straddled my middle, rubbing her pussy along my cock, raised her bottom, reached down to hold my cock upright and pressed herself down over me. I reveled in the feeling of being swallowed by her slick moist heat perceptible even through the latex. We both sighed as her buttocks pushed tight against my thighs. I was running my hands over her belly, delighting in the crisp fleeciness of the curly black hair, following it to where it reached an apex at her navel.

"You do like hair, don't you?" She said, leaning over, squashing her boobs against my chest like two soft pillows, and kissing my face with soft pecks before seeking out my mouth. I was stroking her thighs and ass to feel the mossy fuzz. "You're a funny man," she said, sitting up and moving on me. "A lot of guys don't even seem to notice it, or ignore it, and some think it's a turn-off. I haven't met many who like it the way you do."

I began fondling her bobbing breasts, teasing the thick nipples, as we smiled into each other's eyes. We'd found a slow, pleasing, rhythm. She'd lift up off me until only the head of my cock remained inside her and then descend, making my full length disappear into her pink warmth. As she reached bottom I'd push up to meet her till we'd achieved maximum connection. "Hmmm," she'd sigh. And then lift off me again.

I looked over to see what Annie and Cassie were doing. Cassie was lying on her back with her eyes closed while Annie crouched over her kissing and sucking her breasts and nipples. I watched Annie move downward, rubbing her cheek on the fuzz of Cassie's belly. As Annie neared her pussy Cassie spread her legs; I caught a glimpse of glistening pinkness just before Annie's red head blocked my view .

Heather must have seen the amazement on my face. "You didn't know your wife was a cunnivore?" She asked. Cassie laughed quietly, her eyes still closed. Annie grinned at me over Cassie's belly. I could see her arm moving and knew her fingers must be sliding into Cassie's pussy.

"Do you remember Laura?" My wife asked.

Did I remember Laura? Laura had been Annie's roommate in college and, about two years after Annie and I had first gotten together, she'd come on to me at a party while Annie was out of town, visiting her parents. I spent the night at her apartment. Later I learned that Annie had told Laura that if she was interested in being with me she, Annie, wouldn't mind. Laura and I got together several times after that first night.

"Laura.?" I said.

"Yes, dear, Laura. More than a few times. We were living in the same room, after all."

"Cunnilingus. Lingus means tongue. Annie must be bi-lingual," Cassie said in an affected voice. Heather and Annie groaned.

I was busy attempting to remember all the times that Laura, Annie and I had been together socially, trying to recall if there had been any sign of their intimacy. Nothing came to mind.

Heather, who'd paused during the conversation, now began to move again. She was moving faster, with more concentration. Her eyes closed. I wiggled my finger through the mass of black curls and found the button of her clit. She opened her eyes, smiled at me, and then closed them again.

Cassie's hand reached out to stroke my arm. When I looked at her I saw that her eyes were shut. I caught her hand and her fingers intertwined with mine. She gave my hand a squeeze. I dropped my gaze to Annie's bobbing head,

"Oh." Cassie sighed. I saw her stomach undulate.

The sound of Cassie's expression of pleasure seemed to stir Heather's desire. She began to ride me harder. "Ugh." she cried as she smacked down on me. "Ugh." she cried again.

All of a sudden everyone's mood had become deadly serious. It was as if we'd been transformed from joggers bouncing along with light camaraderie into sprinters straining every sinew to cross the finish line. "Oh God, Annie." Cassie moaned, gripping my hand tight. I watched her, mesmerized by the flow of emotions moving swiftly across her face. A powerful energy field seemed to vibrate in the air.

Heather seemed transfigured. She hooked her hands around the sides of my chest and struggled up on her feet, maintaining our connection, until she was crouching over me with her bottom in the air. I was fascinated by the sight of the stalk of my cock rising up to disappear into her forest of hair. Once she was in position she began to thump down on me with smacking jolts. "Oh fuck." She grunted through her teeth. Her face was screwed up in what looked like terrible pain. Smack. "Oh fuck." Smack. "Oh fuck."

I felt the first telltale tingling signs of orgasm. "Oh yeah, fuck me; you're gonna make me come," I groaned. Cassie gave my hand a hard squeeze and I squeezed back.

"Oh, oh, oh, oh God. Oh Annie." Cassie cried out beside me. It was clear she was in the throes of a climax. Heather picked up the pace and I began rising to meet her, our bodies coming together with spanking noises. It took us a few moments to get the rhythm right but once we did we pounded together in synchronized motion, each impact carrying us a little closer to release. Both of us were grunting and moaning. Heather seemed to reach a point of excitement where she couldn't control the rhythm and we went out of sync. I was very close and the disruption frustrated me. Almost without thinking, and rather roughly, I struggled up and pushed her over on her back. She was looking at me with a fierce abandoned grin.

"You want me to make you come? Would you like that?" I grunted vehemently. Without waiting for an answer or expecting one I grabbed her thighs and spread her open, gaping at the thick carpet of black hair that covered her pussy and belly. Then I was inside her. Grasping her thighs I pulled her toward me, fucking her with urgent, needy, strokes. I jammed my right hand down between us and found her clit. "Come on, baby. Come on." She was staring into my eyes with a feral intensity. Then her eyes closed. Seeking better leverage, I moved on top of her, wrapping my left arm around her shoulders.

"Ahh," she moaned. I fucked her with a kind of perverse deliberation. I knew she was close. I was too. "Ah, Ah," she moaned again. I began vibrating my hand as rapidly as I could, stimulating her pussy's dewy flesh. "Oh yes. Yes. Yes," she cried. "Oh God, yes." A moment later I too was coming. We collapsed together in a sweaty heap.

It was several long minutes before I withdrew from her. Leaning on my elbow I kissed her nose. And when she opened her eyes and pursed her lips I kissed her mouth. It was a tender kiss, quiet and friendly. I turned over on my back, keeping my right hand on her belly, and found Annie's legs stretched out beside me. I ran my other hand up Annie's leg, over her butt, and then wormed two of my fingers into her pussy.

"Hmm," Annie said, wiggling her behind.

Cassie sat up and caressed Annie's head, running her fingers through the short red hair. "I think we should all jump on Annie now." Cassie said. "She's the only one who hasn't come yet."

I withdrew my fingers from Annie's pussy and sat up. "Roll over, Hon," I said, tugging at her hip. She complied. Cassie adjusted herself to take Annie's head in her lap and then bent over to lick one of Annie's nipples, her pink tongue swirling around the areola. Sitting beside her I stroked Annie's thigh. At the touch of my hand she opened her legs wide. I gazed at the familiar landscape of her red haired pussy and then began to run my fingertips over the delicate inner flesh. With a little cry she lifted her butt to meet me. I investigated the mouth of her cunt and found that she was soft and slick. I looked up and saw that Cassie was watching the play of my fingers. "Our little Annie is very very hot," I said. Cassie's eyes met mine and I saw something unfathomable in her expression as well as an openness. Keeping my fingers in Annie's pussy I leaned over. Cassie met me halfway and our lips came together, our tongues mingled. I could have sworn her mute mouth was asking me a question.

As Cassie and I kissed I sensed Heather stirring behind me and then felt her tugging at my hand, signaling me to withdraw it. Heather's face pressed into Annie's crotch and I took the opportunity to run my fingers through Heather's hair and rub the soft skin of her back. Annie began crying out with soft sighing moans.

I was feeling something I'd never felt before in my life. Part of it came from the look, and then the kiss, that had passed between Cassie and me. Part of it was sparked by the velvet texture of Heather's hair under my palm. And then there were Annie's yelps of sensual pleasure. Something about sharing this experience with two other people who were open to exploring the full range of possibilities had brought a new reality into my life. It was as if I'd sunk a shaft to the wellspring of tenderness and the flow now bathed my heart.

Cassie broke off our kiss and once again bent over to suck one of Annie's nipples into her mouth. I fastened my mouth over the other one. Annie's hand began to grope my body, in search of something. What she found was limp with a semen-heavy condom hanging from it. She pulled off the condom and stroked my wet cock.

"Baby, I need you inside me," Annie said with an edge of desperation.

"Come here Mark," Cassie said. I looked at her for a moment, not understanding her intention. "I'll make you hard," she said. I moved to her side, walking on my knees. Annie was looking up, watching; Cassie sucked me into her mouth. Almost at once I began to stiffen. Cassie made ring of her thumb and forefinger and massaged the shaft. Within a minute I had a full erection.

"I need you inside me," Annie repeated.

Cassie let go and I moved into place on my knees. Heather sat up and looked at me. I lifted Annie's legs straight up and laid down on my side, perpendicular to her body. Annie dropped one leg over my thighs and the other over my waist. Heather moved up, her furry pubes pressing against my behind, and reached over to help guide my cock into Annie's pussy.

"Oh. That feels good," Annie sighed.

When I withdrew, Heather leaned over, licked the point where my cock entered Annie's cunt, and then found Annie's clit. Cassie was busy sucking one of Annie's breasts while fondling the other one with her fingers. Heather sat up and I began to fuck with long steady strokes. Heather caressed my butt and watched my cock slide in and out of Annie's pussy.

"That's pretty," Heather said. Cassie glanced up and murmured assent. It felt a little odd to have an audience while making love to my wife but, in a bizarre way, it also felt natural. There was a sweet warmth in sharing this intimacy.

Cassie, teasing Annie's nipples between her thumbs and forefingers, bowed over to offer one of her breasts to Annie's mouth. Heather, meanwhile, had begun to dabble in the area around Annie's clit with her fingertips. I continued the firm steady strokes. Annie was caught in a complex interplay of loving attentions. She didn't have a chance.

"Oh God. Oh God. I can't stand it," she moaned, shuddering and jerking after only a minute or two. In an unspoken agreement the three of us continued our ministrations and, in another minute or so, Annie came again. And again. She was limp with a deep relaxation when we stopped, covered with a fine sheen of perspiration.

Heather, Cassie and I smiled at each other. We were rather proud of ourselves. Heather lay down and snuggled against me, pressing her breasts against my back and putting her arm around my waist. Cassie lay down next to Annie. We all dozed off.

We managed to get up in time to catch the tail end of the evening meal. It seemed strange to be sitting across from Heather and Cassie again, twenty-four hours after meeting them, and be on such different terms of intimacy. All four of us were playing footsie under the table and exchanging delighted, sparkle-eyed, looks above it as we ate and talked. There was a joyous free and easy flow of affection and sexual play among us. Annie and I were concerned at first about how the other people in the camp would react to our unusual bond but Heather and Cassie assured us that these were very tolerant people regarding relationships and this proved to be true. Later, the comments we heard simply reflected the fact that we were viewed as a quartet without any negative implications.

While we were eating, the low throbbing sound of drums began to emanate from the woods, some distance away. Cassie and Heather explained that dancing around a bonfire to the beat of drums was a regular feature of these gatherings. Annie and I were both less than feverous with enthusiasm but it was clear that our two companions were eagerly anticipating the event so we quickly finished eating and joined them in finding the path that led to the constant thumping beat that called to us out of the gathering dark. We got closer and I felt the sonorous pounding quickening my blood and deepening my breath, touching something buried within.

They'd neglected to mention that most of the dancers danced naked so it was a bit of a shock for me when the bonfire came into sight and we saw the flashing forms of a number of naked men and women circling around it, moving to the insistent pounding cadence of the handmade Native American style drums. Heather and Cassie pulled off their dresses as soon as we reached the circle of people watching the dancers. Annie wasn't far behind. I however, chose to remain with the other spectators.

Heather was the hairiest woman among them. I enjoyed watching her dance. She seemed to melt into the intoxicating rhythm, oblivious to the wild swinging of her breasts. I was enthralled by the shifting views of her hairiness revealed by the fire's wavering light.

Cassie was more sedate, less absorbed. I enjoyed watching her too. Her hairiness, I realized, was almost as extensive as Heather's but much lighter, more subtle. Annie, my darling wife, was her usual spritely self and danced with quick joyful leaps. I saw that the three of them maintained an awareness of each other through playful touches and glances.

After observing the variety of movements and soaking up the primal excitement of the drums I found the courage to shuck off my t-shirt and cut-offs and join the exultant throng. The three women noticed my presence and each greeted me with a smile or pat. It was a new experience in a weekend crammed with fascinating new experiences. I would never have imagined how exhilarated I could feel dancing naked with a bunch of other naked people around a fire in the woods to the solid hammering pulse of drums.

We danced for almost six hours, taking occasional breaks to sit on the grass with the spectators and other weary dancers. Finally Cassie announced that she'd had enough. I was ready to go too but both Heather and Annie were caught up in the fever of the dance.

"You guys go back to the tent and we'll show up when we show up, okay?" Annie said.

So Cassie and I put on our clothes and fumbled our way along the pitch black path. "We should have brought flashlights," Cassie grumbled irritably, at one point. For the most part, however, we were silent. I sensed that she was absorbed in her own thoughts and I didn't feel much like talking myself. I felt tired and yet light-hearted. When we got back to the tent we lit the propane lantern only long enough to take off our clothes again and arrange the bedclothes. There was an inexplicable tension between us that nibbled at the back of my mind but didn't capture my full attention. I assumed that something was bothering her. After seeing that she was settled I shut off the lantern and lay down a couple of feet away.

"Good night, Mark," Cassie's voice said out of the darkness.

"Good night, Cassie," I said.

I was balanced on the edge of consciousness, ready to tip over into sleep, when I sensed her moving beside me. "Mark?"

"Hunghh," I responded, swimming up through a series of muddled thoughts.

"I'm sorry, I didn't know you were asleep. Never mind."

"I'm awake now," I said, although that wasn't precisely true.

"I was wondering," she said, trailing off into a long pause.

"What is it Cassie?" I asked gently, my mind coming into focus.

"Mark, would you like to make love to me?" She said in one breath.

Tired as I was the aphrodisiac of a woman's expression of willingness had an effect. I turned toward her, stretching out my hand. She was lying on her side, facing me, and my hand touched the swell of her hip. "Yes, I would," I said. Her hand reached under my arm and discovered my limp cock. "But it may take a little effort. I'm tired."

I leaned towards her and my lips nudged her face in the dark. In response she rolled over on her back. Then my lips covered hers. It was a soft, sweet, kiss. I ran my hand over her belly, enjoying the mossy feel of her hairiness, and then cupped her crotch. She opened her legs and her mouth grew warm. I dipped a finger into the delicate groove and felt her hips lift. I began kissing her earlobes and neck.

"Oh yeah," she breathed, "I like that."

I moved down to find each of her sweet puffy nipples with my mouth. And then I moved her arm so I could push my nose into her pit.

"I'm pretty stinky from the dancing," she said apprehensively.

"I like it," I said, "you smell good. That's one of the things I like about hair."

She laughed in disbelief. "Heather's right. You are a funny man."

"I love loving women the way they are."

"Well, you're sweet. Annie's lucky. But you're still a funny man."

I continued to move down her body, rubbing my cheek on the soft hair of her belly and pussy, until I was crouching in the V of her spread legs. Settling on my stomach I began to shower the insides of her thighs with soft kisses. I'd start at her knee and work my way towards her pussy, pause, and then move down to her other knee.

"You're a goddamned tease," she said the second time I did this.

"Hmmm," I said. I began moving up her thigh a third time. Pause.

"Oh yeah." She sighed as she felt my tongue insinuating itself into the folds of her inner lips. I savored the rich musky scent of her, the first tangy taste. I pushed my hands under her bottom and pulled her furry pussy open with my thumbs. Very gently, with the tip of my tongue, I found the knobby button of her clitoris. "Oh Mark! Oh that feels good." She sighed. After exploring the area around her clit for several moments I slid down the channel between her inner lips, flicking my tongue from side to side, until I discovered the mouth of her vagina which I probed as far as my tongue would go. Then I made the slippery trek back up to her clit. I repeated this circuit again and again. At first there was no sign of a response. And then I felt a faint fluttering in her stomach muscles. Later, as my tongue made a tight circle around her clitoris she caught the back of my head with her hand. "Oh," she moaned.

At this point I concentrated on her clit and, at the same time, inserted my forefinger into her pussy and began moving it in and out. I could sense that she was close.

"Oh God Mark." She started pushing herself up against my mouth. Between her hand at the back of my head and her jerking hips it was getting hard to maneuver but I did what I could. She was very close. With my finger still inside her I opened my mouth and began rubbing the flat surface of my whole tongue, in rapid sweeping movements, across the face of her vulva.

"Oh, oh, oh God. Oh Mark." She rocked her hips hard against me. Clenched tight. Trembled. And then subsided into a pool of relaxation. I moved up her body, kissing her on the way. I paid special attention to her nipples and then covered her mouth with mine. "Hmmm," she said, caressing my ribcage. "Thank you, sweetie," she said when I moved on to kiss her neck and earlobes.

"You're quite welcome," I said.

She reached underneath me and found my cock. What there was of it.

"I don't know if I'm capable of doing anything more," I said.

"Let me see what I can do," she said, "come on, lie down." Once she was positioned between my legs she began rubbing her head against my belly and crotch, her hair whispering on my skin. Then I felt the warmth of her mouth close over my soft cock as her fingers played with my balls. I ran my fingers through her hair. She was batting the head of my cock around with her tongue. I felt the stirring of an erection. She began bobbing up and down on the lengthening shaft. "I love to feel a man's cock get hard in my mouth," she said, lifting her head for a moment. In another minute I was erect. With my cock still in her mouth she began feeling around on the bed until she found what she was looking for. My wet cock stood in the cool air for an instant before I felt her rolling the condom down over it. I smiled in the dark. She must have planned this.

"Fuck me, Mark," she said, lying down beside me and opening her legs. I scrambled up until I was kneeling over her. Her hand caught me and pulled me towards her until I felt the head of my cock engulfed in warmth. I pressed the full length of my cock inside her in one smooth thrust. "Oh God yes." She moaned. I grabbed her knees and pushed them up until they were pressing against the sides of her breasts which lifted her pussy to the right level. I began thrusting into her with an almost demonic concentration. Not fast. Not hard. But with a passionate attention.

"God it feels good to fuck you," I grunted through clenched teeth, "your cunt is so hot and creamy. Do you like how I'm fucking you?"

"Yes," she moaned.

I pulled out until only the head of my cock was inside. "Do you want me to stop? "

"No," she moaned.

"What do you want me to do?" I asked.

"Fuck me, Mark. Goddamn it. Fuck me."

I began thrusting into her again. Faster this time, with more urgency. The only sound was the rapid patta pat of our bodies smacking together. I took my right hand off her knee and started rubbing my thumb around her clitoris. It threw me off balance a bit although I managed to maintain my pace for several thrusts. Then my back gave out. I fell onto her, catching myself on my elbows.

"Did you come?" She asked.

"No, my back hurts. We need to change positions."

"Are you okay?"

"Yeah," I said. I started moving inside her. "This feels better." I wrapped my arms around her shoulders and bent down to kiss her. She met me with an open passionate mouth. I kept fucking her with long deep thrusts. I felt the tingle of my approaching orgasm.

"Play with yourself," I said.

"What?"

"Make yourself come." I felt her hand moving down between our bellies. We were kissing again, moaning into each other's mouths. My climax glided in on a smooth hot track.

"Oh, oh, oh God." She cried. "Oh yes. Oh God." I rode through the choppy waves of her delight as my own release drew closer and closer. Then, as hers subsided, I came with a groan and ground to a halt.

I cradled her in my arms and kissed her sweat-damp cheeks and brow. "That was nice. Thank you." I said.

"Hmmmm," was her response.

I pulled away from her, skinned the condom off my cock and deposited it in the garbage bag. After drying myself with a washcloth I laid down beside her. She was lying on her side so I snuggled up to her backside, spoon fashion. She made a quiet sound of pleasure when I began stroking her skin but a minute or two later I realized she was asleep. I lay in the dark with my arm around her waist. My heart was full of a feeling of deep tenderness as well as a sense of gratitude to these three women for opening themselves to me and to each other so fearlessly. It was like heaven, I thought. I had to laugh, quietly. Certainly if there was anything like heaven in any realm of human experience this was how I'd like it to be.

Sometime later I heard voices, female voices that came closer and closer. Then I could hear them clearly enough to tell that they belonged to Annie and Heather. For an instant I wondered if I should pull away from Cassie and then decided not to. My next dilemma was whether or not I should greet them when they came in. I chose to play 'possum. They fumbled a bit getting into the tent and then I was aware of lantern light.

"I told you they'd do it," Heather said.

"Yeah," my wife said enigmatically.

"Poor babies looks as if they wore themselves out,"

Heather said. Annie didn't reply. "I think Cassie's a bit stuck on your husband," Heather said after a long pause.

"I think you're right," Annie said, "and he isn't pushing her away." There was a pause twice as long as the first.

"Does it bother you?" Heather asked.

Annie gave a deep sigh. "I like Cassie a lot," she said, "but I can't help being a little afraid. But I can't insist on my own freedom and deny Mark his."

"For what it's worth," Heather said, "Cassie likes you too and I don't think she wants to hurt anyone or take Mark away from you."

"We'll have to see what happens. This is all pretty new," my wife said.

There was the rustle of clothes being removed and then the lantern went out. After a few moments of silence there was a distinct sigh of pleasure. I fell asleep to the sound of their sexual play.

I woke up to find myself surrounded by a delightful landscape of naked female bodies. Cassie, on my left and nearest to me, was on her stomach with her hands pushed under the pillow under her head. I reached out to stroke her bottom and lower back. She mumbled something, shifted her position a little, and then opened her eyes.

"Good morning," I said.

"Hungh." She said and closed her eyes.

I heard movement behind me and rolled over on my other side. Annie was watching me. I leaned over to give her a kiss. "Good morning, darling. How are you doing?"

"I'm having some problems," she said with a little grimace, "but let's talk about it later."

Heather stirred. "Good morning everybody," she said.

"Good morning," Annie and I responded. The three of us talked quietly about last night's dancing. Both Annie and I expressed our wonder at how powerfully we'd been moved by the experience.

Heather told us that it had been a good night of drumming. Annie said that she and Heather hadn't gotten in until after three a.m. After we'd been talking for awhile Cassie woke up and joined us.

"If we're going to get any breakfast we'd better get going," Heather said at last. At this we all roused ourselves and began dressing.

"I don't know about you guys but I could use a shower." Cassie stated. "When I can smell myself I know it's bad."

This created the agenda for the next three hours. We did manage to find some breakfast although we were among the last to arrive. And after eating we walked down to the shower area and took over one of the open stalls. We were like four kids, splashing, laughing and soaping each other's backs. There was a warm interplay of jokes, transparent glances, and physical contact. I detected a certain amount of tension, and a sense of distance, between Annie and Cassie but neither seemed to be so caught up in their feelings that they were unable to join in.

"Annie, would it be all right with you if Mark and I go for a little walk?" Heather asked. The four of us were in the last stages of toweling ourselves off.

"I'm not his keeper," my wife said, "so yeah, it's okay."

Heather looked at me and I responded with an affirmative shrug and a questioning look. She gave me a smile and turned back to Annie and Cassie. "And I think it would be a good idea for the two of you to have a talk before things get out of hand." Cassie's face showed a hint of color as she looked at Annie; Annie sighed but nodded. Heather folded a large towel and draped it across her shoulder. "Come on Mark," she said, taking my hand. Still naked, except for our sandals and a small pouch that Heather carried, we took one of the paths leading out of the meadow and into the trees.

For a time we were both silent, connected by our handclasp and the sounds of our footsteps and breathing. I walked beside her feeling mystified.

"Annie has been singing your praises ever since I met her," Heather said, breaking the silence. I made a short strangled laugh that was meant to indicate modesty. "But I have to say I thought you sounded too good to be true. I was very curious to meet you." She gave me a sideways smiling glance and then said. "I don't know if all the things she's told me are correct but I do know I like you. I like you a lot."

"I like you too," I said.

"And I wanted to tell you how much I've appreciated the way you've accepted me." She fell silent for a time and I could sense her struggling to put her feelings into words. "It hasn't been easy for me to feel good about myself," she said in a low voice, rough with emotion, "for a bunch of reasons I'm not going to go into. But I've done it, even though it's not always easy. Shit still comes up sometimes."

"That's true for everyone," I said, "we've all got our stuff. It makes life interesting."

"Yeah, you're right," she said with a pained laugh. "But what I'm trying to say is that I appreciate how I feel around you." She stopped and our eyes met. "I like the way you look at me, Mark. I've seen the way you've looked at my body. I've seen how turned on you get. And it goes deeper than my being hairy, I know it does."

I felt myself blush and licked my lips. "I like women, I guess."

"Yeah, I think you do. It's funny. Annie's a skinny little thing who can't grow hair for shit but the love the two of you have for each other is so thick you can almost cut it with a knife. I'm so envious of her I could scream." She said this with humor but there was an edge to her amusement. "And yet you respond to me more than any man has for a long time." Once more I sensed the pain within her moving close to the surface and put my arms around her, feeling her large breasts press against me. "No, no, it's okay," she said into my neck before pulling away. She took my hand again and we continued up the path.

Several minutes later she guided me off the path and through a patch of undergrowth; almost magically we came upon a small grassy area surrounded by trees. "I found this the first day we were here," she said. "Cassie and I were hiking and I needed to pee so I went behind those bushes and voila." She spread the towel on the thick grass and sat down and I sat beside her. Neither of us seemed to have any doubt about why we were there and a moment later my lips had found hers. She leaned back and I followed her. There was a quality of tenderness and intimacy that hadn't existed earlier as well as a lack of urgency. We kissed for a long time, exploring each other's mouth; from time to time we'd pause to gaze into one another's eyes. At the same time our hands were stroking the contours of each other's body.   Finally, after opening a condom she'd taken from her pouch and rolling it over my cock, she opened her legs and I slipped in between them.

"Oh, that feels good," I sighed. My cock slid into her enveloping warmth. She murmured affirmatively. I moved slowly, holding myself above her on extended arms, gazing into her eyes. A profound openness blossomed between us. We didn't seem to be moving in the usual pattern of build up and release. This seemed more like a growing flow of energy. We moved together for a long time, exploring this slow sweet union. The sky had been cloudy most of the day with brief moments of sunlight breaking through now and then. So what happened next took on the aspect of a minor miracle. I was continuing to thrust and withdraw while gazing into her eyes. At times I'd look down at the mass of hair on her belly and pubic region and watch my latex covered cock, which gleamed with her juices, disappear from sight.

It was while I was entranced by the sight of my belly pressing against her mossy black fuzz that she spoke. "Mark, look." I followed her gaze and saw a large multicolored butterfly resting on a flower beside us, beating its wings. "A messenger," she said reverently, "it's come to tell us something." At that very moment a shaft of sunlight broke through the clouds and illuminated the glade. This combination of events triggered something. I felt as if my consciousness had expanded to take in all creation. My cock felt as if it were miles away in some other world and yet every sensation touched my nerves with a powerful immediacy. Each stroke seemed to resonate with the rhythms of the cosmos. From a great distance I heard Heather crying out and then a deep, oceanic, pulsing flowed through me into her and then through her into me. It was like nothing I'd ever experienced before. And then my consciousness shrank back into the confines of my flesh.

Heather was staring at me. I was staring at her. "Did you feel it too?" She asked at last, tentatively. All I could do was nod in wonder. At the same instant we looked toward the flower. The butterfly was gone.

We were both shaken, awestruck. Wordlessly we gathered up the towel and pouch and returned to the path, making our way down to the large meadow. By some unspoken agreement neither of us said anything to Annie or Cassie when we joined them although I did tell Annie later, after we'd gotten home.

But as it happened our two companions weren't in a state of mind to pick up on our reticence. As soon as we saw them it was clear that the tensions between them had been resolved, at least for the time being. They were sitting side by side at the camp table, Cassie in her yellow sundress and Annie naked, with their heads bent together and their hands clasped. Heather gave me a swift twinkling look before we made our presence known.

"You two look happy," Heather said. They looked up with bright open smiles on their faces and got to their feet. Seconds later they were both hugging me and each other. Over their shoulders I could see Heather looking on with a bemused smile.

"We had a good talk." Annie said, "I feel silly about getting so bent out of shape.

"You felt what you felt," Cassie said severely, "we all get afraid sometimes. You shouldn't be so hard on yourself."

"I know. I know," Annie said, wrinkling her nose at Cassie. "I still feel silly though." Cassie leaned over and kissed her lightly.
"We need to get going," I said. A veil of sadness fell over us for an instant.

"But we'll see you in the city," Cassie said brightly. "This is only the beginning, isn't it?" We all glanced around at the others.

"I know I hope it is," Annie said, "this was a very special weekend for me.

"For me too." The rest of us said in turn.

Annie and I started to gather our stuff together and pack the car while Heather and Cassie kept us company. When it came time to take down the tent they helped us squeeze it down into a reasonably small bundle and jam it in the trunk of the car. At last we were ready. We all said goodbye with long hugs and tender kisses and then Annie and I climbed into our overstuffed vehicle and drove away, waving farewell. I put my hand on her knee and our eyes met. We didn't need to say a word.

Song For Maria

Juan Gutierrez was restless. Maria, his wife, had gone to Mexico for a month-long visit with her parents and siblings. That was three weeks ago and he missed her terribly. She was the heart and soul of his life. He missed her cheerful bustling around the apartment. He missed the flash of her eyes. He missed her full strong laughter in the face of all life's problems. He missed her body.

How he missed her body. Her rich brown skin. Her deep brown hair. The wave-like sway of her breasts. The earthy swing of her bottom. He yearned for another of those mornings when he could lie in bed and watch her move around the room naked, in the light of the new sun. He loved her so much. Seeing her was food for his soul. Making love with her was a banquet of all the bounty of the earth and the deep waters of the spirit spiced with laughter and intense sensation. She was the only person who brought the purpose of life into clear focus for him.

He picked up his violin from its stand not far from the open window. He was a very accomplished musician. In his mind he'd been working on a composition for his Maria and he longed to play it for her. He began to play it now. He felt the deep power of his longing enter his fingers and he played as he'd never played before.

The apartment building in which Juan Gutierrez lived was an old one and the sounds of his passionate hunger, translated into music, moved out and into windows, slipped through cracks, slid through air ducts, and made the walls and floors resonate. And all those who heard his song of desire were deeply moved.

In the apartment below, Annie De Pauw, a wounded and lonely single woman with a long string of failed relationships, was lying in bed reading. She was struggling to hold the quart container of ice cream and keep the book open with one hand while using the other hand to spoon ice cream into her mouth. Her four cats were sprinkled around the bedspread. Moments after the strains of Juan's music entered her consciousness trembling tears began to slide down her face.

Next door Don and Ashley Klingendorfer, a couple in their 60s, with almost 40 years of marriage behind them, were watching TV. It was when Don hit the mute button on the remote that they became aware of the thrilling intensity of sound flowing in through their partly opened window. They looked across the room at each other. It was as if they were seeing the other's face for the first time.

In the ground floor apartment furthest from Juan's, Russell Carter, a man living with his lover Bill Mosher, was surfing the Internet for images of gay porn. He often did this when Bill was at work; sitting naked for hours in front of the monitor with his cock in one hand while he used the mouse to navigate with the other. He was the last to become aware of the powerful music. When he did he went into the dark kitchen to open the window to hear better. It filled him with a mix of strong emotions.

At this point Juan wasn't playing the parts in sequence. There were several that he felt needed work and he focused on them to see if he could find the perfect melodic phrasing. Due to the strength of his longing for Maria, and with the image of her beauty in his mind, he found that the ideas flowed easily and clicked into place. A wild exhilaration began to grow inside him as he felt a rush of creative power he'd never experienced before.

Annie was sobbing. She'd put the ice cream on the nightstand and the book on the bedspread. Her four companions were looking at her in alarm. She pushed back the bedspread, swung her legs out, and stood. She felt all stirred up. She didn't know why she was crying. Her body was flooded with all the signs of sexual arousal for no reason she could find. Her hands pulled at her nightdress, bunching it up in her fingers. She wondered if she was going crazy. Then she had to be naked. Usually she didn't like to be naked. To see herself. But it seemed okay now. She wanted to see herself. She pulled the nightdress over her head and threw it on the floor.

Don and Ashley looked at each other. Theirs had been a largely nonphysical relationship for a number of years but now the old fire flashed between them. Don felt himself becoming erect, something that hadn't happened in a long time.

"Juan's getting that piece worked out," Don said. He'd been a high school music teacher and often talked to Juan about composition.

"I'm horny," Ashley said.

"Me too," her husband said. "I'm even getting hard."

"Oh yeah?" His wife said. "This I gotta see." She crossed the room, knelt down beside Don's armchair, and pulled down the zipper of his pants. Squirreling around in his boxers she found the prize and lifted it into view. "God lover, it's beautiful." Don felt very proud of himself.

Ashley leaned over and took him in her mouth. She'd forgotten how much she'd enjoyed this. She loved hearing Don's moans of pleasure. She felt his fingers running through her hair.

The urge to be naked struck them both at the same time. Don struggled out of the chair and Ashley rose to her feet with some difficulty. They laughed together at the awkwardness of trying to get out of their clothes quickly. Soon they were looking at their partner's body, the body they'd known for so long. But tonight there was something different.

Russell was standing in the darkness in confusion. He'd immediately sensed the erotic energy pulsing in the music Juan was making but his thoughts weren't going where he was trying to guide them. He was trying to bring up the images he'd seen on his computer monitor but over and over his thoughts returned to Bill, his lover. For almost a year he'd felt closed in by his relationship with Bill. He'd begun to think about all the men he would never know in a sexual way. He felt he was missing something. So it confused him now to find himself thinking of the intimate moments he and Bill had shared. He was unable to hold the image of another man in his mind for more than a second or two. He stubbornly resisted the flow of his thoughts until, realizing the futility of his efforts, he relaxed.

At this moment he became aware of his nakedness. He moved into the light that flowed from the living room and enjoyed the ebony hues of his skin.

Juan, eager to capture all the new ideas he'd just generated, turned on his digital recording equipment and began to play his new composition in its entirety. As he played he felt as if his soul connected with Maria's and now she was with him. His spirit went into another world while his body continued to play the violin in this one.

Annie was once again sitting up in her bed, her back against the headboard. But now she was naked. She ran her hands over her body. Rivulets of tears poured down her face and fell onto her breasts. Liquid diamonds of compressed pain were being washed out of her, leaving space for something else. She almost never masturbated but now she began to. She spread her legs and explored. Now that the pain was out of her body it felt good. It felt very good. She spread her legs wider.

Ashley had led Don to the couch and then reclined on her back, opening herself to him. He touched her, feeling her wetness. This too hadn't happened for a long time. On the rare occasions they made love they had to use an artificial lubricant. He had two fingers inside her, delighting in her obvious arousal. They looked into each other's eyes and saw their own wonder and passion reflected there. He knelt between her knees and entered her.

"Oh honey, that feels so good," Ashley sighed. "Oh God, it feels good."

Russell began stroking his cock. He went to his computer and tried pulling up one of the images he'd been excited by earlier but it didn't interest him. It was like an old piece of gum with all the flavor chewed out. He turned off the computer and thought of Bill, of all they'd shared together. Of how much they meant to each other. He stroked himself more vigorously as the images flowed through his mind, images filled with warmth, and passion, and tenderness. He was amazed at how turned on he was. The feelings of arousal in response to what he'd seen on the Internet paled in comparison.

Juan found himself observing his physical body as if it was one small part of his totality. He was aware of a power he'd never known before flowing through him, out into the world. He listened, as if from a distance while knowing no distance existed, as the part of himself playing the violin began the final movement.

Annie was fingering herself frantically, caught up in the pleasure that sped like tingles of electricity through her belly. She felt herself moving towards orgasm. Her tears had subsided for the most part but there were still lingering flashes of pain and fear. At the moment they struck she would lose her momentum for several seconds and she'd feel her orgasm recede. But the music carried her past these interruptions. She sensed her climax drawing closer and closer and a new, and almost alien, feeling began to fill the space where the pain had been. Hope. It flooded in, pouring into her heart. Now she was crying again but these were tears of joy. And then her orgasm was there. She was yelling but didn't know it. She was crying out in celebration.

Don and Ashley clutched each other in delight. They thought they'd forgotten. But they hadn't. They remembered all the special touches, the special moves, the intimate sounds, that created the deepest response in their partner's mind and body. They danced together as they had so many times before when they were younger. But now, it seemed, although their bodies weren't as agile as they'd been, they were connecting at a deeper level than, in their youth, they'd ever dreamed existed. With intuitive certainty they sensed each others passion rising and quickened their movements.

"Kiss me, Oh God, kiss me," Ashley moaned, feeling herself overtaken.

Don leaned down and pressed his mouth to hers. Her lips were hot and urgent. Her tongue tangled with his. She was screaming her pleasure into his mouth. He felt himself erupt.

Russell was sitting in his computer chair with legs spread, leaning back, his eyes closed. He was skirting the edge of orgasm, moving his hand as needed, quickly or slowly, to keep himself there. He was yearning for Bill now. He wondered how he ever could have thought that having sex with a variety of strangers was something important. In his mind he was making love with his dearest Bill. They were looking into each other's eyes, open to the pleasure they shared. His hand was moving faster. He was ready now. "This is for you, Bill. This is for you," he moaned. The white semen pulsed out onto the black skin of his belly.

Juan, returning to this world, pulled the violin from under his chin in a daze. He could only remember fragments of his ecstatic journey. For almost fifteen minutes he stood there, trying to gather himself together. He went over to his recording equipment and skipped to the beginning of the piece he'd just played. Yes, it was there. He marveled at the sound of it. He found it hard to believe that that was him playing. All at once he realized he felt very very tired. Turning off his equipment and the lights he stumbled towards the bedroom.

Annie lay in her bed, very relaxed and at peace. She felt as if a great weight had been lifted. She followed the thoughts that moved like skitter bugs across the water. She thought of Juan and Maria. She'd often seen them together but always a black cloud of pain had fallen over her. All she saw was that they had what she didn't have. And her heart would close. But now, with the pain gone, she realized she needed to find a man like Juan. A man who knew the language of his heart and wasn't afraid to speak. A man very different from the men she'd found herself seeking out in the past. With sudden resolve she sat up. She saw the ice cream on the nightstand and without hesitation dropped it in the wastebasket. A moment later the book, a romance novel, followed. She stood up, liking the feel of her body, and began to pace with growing excitement. She would call her friend Cynthia, she decided. The friend she'd been avoiding for so long because Cynthia would always ask if she was getting out, doing things. Perhaps it was time. Cynthia would know where to start.

Ashley and Don were cuddling, holding each other on the couch and quietly kissing. They hadn't known this kind of contentment for a long time.

"We should ask Juan if we could have a tape of that music so we could play it every night," Don said.

"Every night?" Ashley laughed. "Are you up to satisfying me every night, you old goat?"

"With that music I think I might be."

"Oh God, Don, that would be so wonderful," Ashley sighed, melting. They pulled each other close, seeing the happy tears in the other's eyes.

Russell was whistling as he moved around the apartment. He found the candles, the scented ones, and the massage oil. He cleaned the bedroom and changed it around to create a little bower for love. He placed the candles and prepared the oil, laying a large towel over the comforter. At last it was ready. His Bill was going to be in for a real treat when he got home from work.

Juan lay for a moment at the edge of sleep filled with the exultation of an artist who knows he has found the perfect expression for a particular piece of art. He was unaware how deeply he'd touched the lives of four people, his neighbors. He was totally ignorant of the fact that within three years his recording of "Song For Maria", released initially on a very small label only to be snatched up within two months by the biggest in the business, would radically transform the lives of every person living on this planet.

About the author

Stanfield Major was born in Normal, Illinois. He began writing at the age of fifteen, starting with short unrhymed poems. And then he tried fiction. Novels he didn't finish. About a year later he began writing song lyrics. His creative life has consisted of a restless shifting from one to another of these forms of expression. He's now fifty-four.

In 2002 he began posting to Literotica, an online forum for writers of erotica. Over the next two years he wrote enough erotic short stories to fill a book. The manuscript was submitted to Renaissance Ebooks, in January 13, 2005 and within two weeks it had been accepted.

Stanfield currently resides in Kingman, Arizona and is working on another book of erotic short stories, a romance novel, and plans to produce several CDs of his songs.

You're welcome to email the author at jazm48@yahoo.com and share thoughts, comments, and suggestions. He's always looking for Muses; you could be the satisfied leading lady of his next story.

www.ingramcontent.com/pod-product-compliance
Lightning Source LLC
Chambersburg PA
CBHW030530020726
47494CB00004B/1289